AF390189

Charles Wadsworth Camp

Sinister Island

e-artnow 2020

Charles Wadsworth Camp

Sinister Island

A Supernatural Mystery

e-artnow, 2020
Contact: info@e-artnow.org

ISBN 978-80-273-0853-8

Contents

CHAPTER I
THE DANGEROUS HABITATION

Captain's Island is not far from civilisation as one measures space. Dealing with the less tangible medium of custom, it is-or was-practically beyond perception.

James Miller didn't know this. When he had thought at all of his friend Anderson's new winter home he had pictured the familiar southern resort with hotels and cottages sheltering Hammonds peerage, and a seductive bathing beach to irritate the conservative.

That background, indeed, was given detail by his own desires. For he had received Anderson's letter concerning the new move while still in bed with a wearisome illness. Now, after two months' convalescence in quiet waterways, he was ready to snare pleasure where it was most alluring before returning to the North and Wall Street. So he sent a telegram from Allairville, instructing Anderson to meet him in Martinsburg and conduct him to the revels of his tropical resort. As a matter of fact it was this wire, despatched with such smiling anticipation, that became the leash by which he was drawn into the erratic, tragic, and apparently unaccountable occurrences which at the time added immeasurably to the lonely island's evil fame.

Still it went, and Miller, ignorant of what he faced, went after it as quickly as he could, which was with the speed of a snail. It took his small cruising launch forty-eight hours, including a minimum of rest, to conquer the fifty miles between Allairville and Martinsburg. Because of this aversion of his boat to anything approximating haste he had caused the name Dart to be painted across the stern in arresting letters.

As the droll craft loafed down into the busy roadsteads of the southern metropolis this warm May morning. Miller, in perfect consonance with its bland indifference, lay in a steamer chair on the upper deck. Clothed in white flannels and smoking a pipe, he surveyed with gentle calm a petulant, unreasonable world. He smiled pleasantly at enraged tug-boat and barge captains. Crawling through the railroad drawbridge, he waved a greeting free from malice at the keeper, who, arms akimbo, chin uptilted, bawled his expectations of a train by midnight and his reasonable ambition to clear the draw before that hour.

Nor did the native, leaning against the wheel forward, respond even by a glance to these studied incivilities. His ears seemed to be occupied exclusively by the engine as capricious symptoms; his eyes, by his goal, at last within view; his hands, by the wheel as he coaxed the Dart to the urgencies of traffic.

Miller eyed the fellow approvingly. By rare good luck he had hired him down the state when he had bought this boat as the first ingredient of the doctor's prescription for a long rest in the South. At the start the man had proved his fitness by exposing an abnormal affection for diseased gasoline motors. Since then he had served Miller acceptably as captain, engineer, deck-hand, cook, and, in a sketchy sense, valet. Moreover he knew obscure, uncharted channels. He had a special intuition for the haunts of fish and game. In the villages where they paused for supplies he out-bargained the storekeepers almost without words. Miller appreciated that it was due only to his devotion and ingenuity that the Dart at present indifferently blocked traffic in the river before Martinsburg. With the inexcusable confidence most of us bring to the contemplation of the immediate future he regretted his early parting with this admirable Crichton.

When the Dart was made fast to her appointed place at the dock Miller lowered his legs, arose, and stretched himself to his full height comfortably. He glanced at his watch. It was noon. He had wired Anderson to meet him at the boat at one o'clock. For the first time he realised he had made a thoughtless rendezvous. Why had he not mentioned an hotel? This thriving town might have offered comparative culinary splendour after the plainness to which he had abandoned himself on the Dart. As it was he must offer his hospitality to Anderson at that hour, and Anderson, no doubt, after two months of heavy luxury at his winter resort, would gratefully accept.

"Tony," he said, "you deserve the rest of the day. Why should injustice always trouble the deserving?"

Tony, standing below, leaned his elbows on the break of the upper deck. His eyes behind the bushy brows expressed no positive emotion-certainly not chagrin or revolt.

"I've asked some one to meet me here at one o'clock," Miller went on. "I must offer him luncheon unless you strike, in which case I wouldn't be much annoyed. In fact I'd take you back tonight. Do as you wish. I'm going up-town."

Tony lowered his bearded face and slid down the companionway. Miller stepped to the dock.

"Tony!" he called.

The native thrust his head through the hatch and waited impassively. Miller handed him some silver.

"For what we lack in case your sense of duty throttles commonsense."

A brown hand closed over the money. The emotionless face was withdrawn.

Miller strolled through the city. After his months of exile from so familiar a setting he experienced a sense of elation at the thud of a hard pavement beneath his feet, at the cacophony of street noises, at the air of badly-guarded impatience given out by these men and women who crowded him at the crossings. It was good to be well, to be on the threshold of that vaster, more selfish hubbub of his own city. No more days and nights on the boat in lonely places, he reminded himself. And he was glad.

This was the frame of mind in which he returned to the dock to meet his first dampening and significant disappointment. He saw Tony leaning, sphinx-like, against the rail of the Dart, but there was no sign of Anderson.

"Any word from the guest?" he asked Tony as he came up.

The native drew a crumpled, soiled envelope from his pocket. He handed it over the rail.

As he took the envelope Miller recognised his friend's writing. While he read the brief note a frown drove the satisfaction from his face, leaving bewilderment.

Anderson had commenced in his customary affectionate manner, but beyond that everything was unexpected', puzzling.

"It is far from convenient for me to leave Molly" the letter ran; and Miller could frame no satisfactory explanation for that except the serious illness of Anderson's wife. Yet the rest of the letter said nothing of illness; did not even suggest it.

"For heaven's sake," it went on, "or more strictly for our own, come down to Captain's Island, Jim. Come this afternoon if it is humanly possible. Anchor in the inlet if you can get anybody to steer you through. The channel is hard to negotiate, but you won't find that the chief difficulty in hiring a pilot. I'll watch for you. If you make it I'll row out immediately and tell you the rest. Then you can decide if you want to help us out of this mess and back to commonsense. Molly sends her anxious best."

Miller read the letter twice before returning it to the soiled envelope. The only clear fact was that Anderson and Molly were in trouble. Anderson had written that he would tell him the rest on his arrival. But the rest of what! For he had told him nothing.

"How did this come?" he asked Tony.

The native pointed to a steamboat, diminutive and unkempt, made fast to a neighbouring dock.

"Boy brought it over," he mumbled.

Miller glanced at his watch. Curiosity was useless. His friends needed him. He would leave at the earliest possible moment.

"This letter, Tony," he said, "is unexpected and important. If you've the usual plans of sea-faring men while in port banish them."

He swung on his heel.

"I'll be back in a few minutes."

He hurried from the dock to a telegraph office which he had noticed during his walk. He saw only one operator on duty and he found himself the only patron. He wrote a despatch to

Anderson, saying he was leaving at once, and handed it to the agent, a good-natured young fellow in his shirt sleeves.

The man glanced at the address, raised his eyes quickly to Miller's face, and let the yellow slip flutter to the counter.

"Well!" Miller demanded.

"Can't send that to Captain's Island."

"Place censored or quarantined?" Miller asked impatiently.

"Might as well be quarantined-for the yellow fever," the agent drawled, "but the main point is there isn't any wire there. Of course I can send a messenger boy down on the little boat to Sandport this afternoon. He might get somebody to row him across the river, and he could walk the three miles or so. Sent one down to Mr. Anderson that way yesterday. But this doesn't seem important, and you can figure the expense."

Miller's preconceived notions of Captain's Island began to crumble.

"Not worth it," he said.

"Besides," the agent went on, "it's hard to get anybody to walk that island at night. Since you're going yourself —"

Again he stared curiously and with a sort of wonder at Miller.

"I don't want to pry, but mighty few people go —"

Miller laughed.

"It seems to me my question comes first. What's the matter with Captain's Island?"

The agent picked the yellow form up and handed it to Miller.

"And you ask me I —I don't know. Nobody knows. People been asking that for a good many more years than I am old."

Miller tore the message up. He glanced around the somnolent office.

"I'm not good at riddles either," he said, "but if you'll let me have this one I'll try. You see I'm going there."

The agent shuffled uncomfortably from one foot to the other.

"It's this way," he said at last. "It's all talk, but it's been going on a long while, as I said, and we understand it down here. Now you're from the North. I don't want to make myself a laughing stock!"

Miller smiled. Then he recalled the troubled tone of Anderson's letter and his smile died,

"I promise I won't laugh," he said. "Of course I can guess. Superstition?"

"That's it," the agent answered. "The neg***s and the fishermen around Sandport have given the island a bad name. They won't go near it if they can help themselves, and even the people here have got in the habit of leaving it a wide berth. I went down one Sunday with a crowd of wild boys, and I've never wanted to go back-not that I saw anything. Don't think that. But there's a clammy, damp, unhealthy feeling about the place. I'll say this much: if there's such things as ghosts that's the proper place to look for them."

"Probably climate. Close to the ocean, isn't it?"

"Yes. It's like most of these sea islands-marshes on one side, an inlet on the other, across that, rolling sand dunes for maybe a quarter of a mile, and nothing beyond but the everlasting ocean. They say in the old days it was a hang-out of the buccaneers. And lonely! I can't tell you how lonely that place looks. Besides it's got a bad reputation for rattlesnakes-no worse in the state that I know of, but that isn't why people stay away."

"Superstition," Miller said, "always comes out on top. It's funny how these yarns get started."

"Not so funny when you think of all that's happened on Captain's Island," the agent answered. "Trouble is, everybody knows its history. Guess they scare the children with it still. They did when I was a youngster. I've behaved myself many a time because they said if I didn't old Noyer would chain me up."

"Old Noyer!"

"A giant of a brute from Louisiana, who laid the island out as a plantation in the thirties to raise sea island cotton. They say he carried fifty or sixty slaves, and was a big dealer on the side. Ruins of the quarters are still there if you've got the nerve to go look 'em over. I started, but I didn't get far. The island was a jungle, and I tell you it didn't feel right to me. I'm not superstitious, but you're kind of looking for something all the time there. Anyway, old Noyer was a regular king. He ruled that island and the inlet and that lonely coast. Wasn't accountable to anybody. When the law made it a crime to import any more slaves into the country, he laughed in his sleeve, and ran raving shiploads in just the same. He kept the poor devils prisoners in the quarters until he could scatter the ones that didn't die or go stark crazy around the biggest markets. Those quarters have got a right to be haunted, I reckon. Seems a pure-blooded Arab girl was brought over with a shipload of blacks. They say she was the daughter of a chief, and somebody in Africa had reasons for getting rid of her. Even Noyer didn't dare try to sell her. They say he took a fancy for her, and by and by married her. He built a coquina house for her about a mile and a half from the plantation."

"A coquina house! What's that?"

"Coquina? It's a shell deposit they used a lot in the old days for building, Noyer fixed it up in fine style for this Arab girl. She lived there until one night that giant took it into his head without reason that he ought to be jealous of her. He didn't wait to find out he was wrong. He cut her throat as she lay in bed. That's the house where this man, Mr. Anderson lives-the man you wanted to send the telegram to."

Miller started. Yet he could not accept the agent's story of this ancient crime in Anderson's house as a credible explanation of his friend's note. Anderson and Molly were both normal and healthy. He had been in more or less constant touch with them since he had first met Anderson in Paris ten years before when he had been on the threshold of manhood. During that time he had seen no display of abnormality or of any exceptional surrender to nerves. The question that troubled principally now was why Anderson had ever chosen such a spot.

"You knew then," he asked the agent, "about Mr. Anderson's living there?"

"Sure. It's natural everybody should get wind of that. You see his house and the plantation house are the only two on the island, and until this winter they've both stood empty since the Civil War. Oh, yes, everybody heard of it right away."

"Queer they aren't in ruins, too," Miller said.

"No," the agent explained. " Property's still in the hands of Noyer's family, I believe. They've let it all go back to the wilderness except those two houses. Kept them in repair, figuring, I reckon, somebody might be foolish some day and rent them. Sure enough, this winter along comes a man named Morgan who takes the plantation house, and this man, Mr. Anderson who takes the other. Of the two give me the big place. It's more open and less gruesome than the coquina house. Yes, people would know about that naturally. Been saying Captain's Island would grow civilised again, but I don't hear of any patties going down, and I expect both the Morgans and the Andersons have friends in Martinsburg."

Miller smiled.

"The invasion begins. I'm running down in my small boat this afternoon. How far is it?"

"About twenty-five miles altogether, but if you get a strong tide behind you it doesn't take long."

"My boat needs a water fall."

The agent picked up a paper and turned to the marine page.

"Tide's on the turn now. It runs three to four miles an hour between here and the mouth of the river."

"Then I could make it by night," Miller said. "I suppose I need a pilot?"

"Yes. There's no entrance directly from the river. You have to take a channel across the marshes."

The agent hesitated.

"They call it the Snake."

He cleared his throat, adding apologetically:

"That's because it twists and turns so."

"What about a pilot?" Miller asked.

"Honestly, I don't know," the agent answered. " Might get one to take you by the island in the day time, but I doubt if you can persuade any of these ignorant rivermen to guide you into that inlet at night to anchor."

"That's silly," Miller said irritably.

"Lots of silly things there's no accounting for," the agent replied. "And you can't realise the reputation the island's got around this part of the country. And, see here! Don't you be putting me down as foolish too. I've told you what they say. I don't know anything about spooks-never saw one. All I do claim is, there's a kind of a spell on Captain's Island that reaches out for you and-and sort of scares you. That's all I say —a sort of spell you want to get away from. Maybe you're right and it's just the climate, and that jungle, and the loneliness."

"And I," Miller said, "have been picturing it as a popular winter resort."

"You'll have to ask the snakes and the spooks about that," the agent laughed.

He turned to an entering customer.

Miller went back to the Dart, telling himself that the problem of Anderson's note was as undecipherable as ever. He would have to wait for an explanation until he had seen Anderson that night. Therefore he was all the more anxious to start. He had had enough experience with the natives to accept as final the agent's prophecy about the pilots. Tony, who knew so much river lore, however, might furnish a means if he were handled properly. As soon as he had stepped aboard he called to the man.

The native's bearded face appeared in the companionway. He climbed to the deck, wiping his hands on a ball of waste.

"Tony," Miller said, "do you know the Snake channel?"

Tony started. His hands ceased tearing at the waste.

"It's near the mouth of the river," Miller added.

Tony nodded. He moved uneasily. His eyes questioned.

"Think you could get us through without piling us on an oyster bank?"

The native waited a moment before nodding again with a jerky motion.

These signs were not lost on Miller.

"I've altered my plans," he said. " Instead of abandoning you and the Dart here in a few days as I had intended, I've decided to go a little farther north by water."

Tony's satisfaction was apparent in a smile.

Miller felt it was important to let that impression, which was more or less true, stand-It would explain his desire to navigate the Snake. Once through the Snake and in the inlet he would find ways to laugh Tony out of his superstitious fears.

"So we'll cast off," he said, "and go through the Snake this afternoon."

Tony's smile faded. The bearded lips half opened as though he was about to speak. But his eyes caught the high sun and evidently he changed his mind, for he went down the ladder, and after a moment the engine was indignantly thrashing.

Miller sighed.

Tony reappeared, cast off, took his place at the wheel, and backed the Dart into the river.

Miller seated himself in his deck chair. The city, whose warm, hurried life had just seemed to welcome him, let him go now indifferently to a far greater loneliness than that with which he had thought himself done. He realised this with surprise before three o'clock. The short distance between Captain's Island and the metropolis had deceived him. He had been unable to conceive the desolate nature of that narrow stretch. He had not dreamed of anything like the precipitate loneliness that crowded the last shanty outpost of the great factories.

A little after three the smoke of these factories was a vague haze on the horizon. The high ground on which they stood had fallen abruptly to flat, wet, uninhabitable marshes. These were relieved only by repellent swamps of palmettos or an occasional pine tree which stretched itself, gaunt and gibbet-like, from the waving grass.

Miller's half amused reception of the agent's talk had not been a pose. He had no belief in the supernatural, nor would he admit for an instant that its vapoury rumours would ever have the power to materialise for him into any startling fact Yet this landscape could not fail to impress him as a barren neutral ground between activity and stagnation, between the familiar and the unsounded. It forced him, indeed, to call upon his exceptional will power to fight back a mental inertness, a desire to abandon himself to melancholy. And his will was not altogether victorious. He became ill-at-ease, restless. He glanced at Tony. The native leaned forward, clutching the wheel with both hands as though engaged in a physical attempt to aid the swift tide and the engines. His pipe had, for once, gone out, and remained neglected.

Miller began anxiously to look for signs of the Snake channel. But to either side the dreary marshes swept away apparently unbroken.

At five o'clock, however, Tony turned the Dart towards the left bank of the river. Miller could see a narrow opening in the marsh grass through which glassy water flowed reluctantly. Beyond it, in the direction of the sea, he made out a line of low trees, probably palmettos and cedars. It stretched northward from the river across the marshes for, perhaps, five miles. He pointed at the opening.

"The Snake?" he asked.

Tony nodded. He shifted his feet restlessly. After manipulating his levers until the engine slowed down he faced Miller.

"Anchor?"

Miller arose and walked to the break of the deck.

"Certainly not. I said we were going through the Snake tonight."

Tony shuffled nearer. He spread his hands towards the sky.

"You mean," Miller said, "That it will be dark in an hour or so? I know it. What of it?"

Tony opened his lips. He spoke with painful effort.

"Too late to get past. Would have to anchor by Captain's Island."

He pointed at the low, dense mass of trees which Miller had noticed.

"Naturally," Miller answered. "That's my wish-to anchor in Captain's Inlet."

The threatened change in Tony became complete. It startled. He placed his hands tremblingly on the break of the deck at Miller's feet. His cheeks above the heavy beard had grown white. His eyes showed the first glimmer of revolt Miller had ever detected. But strangest of all, the native, whose habitual silence was broken only by the most imperative demands, burst suddenly into torrential speech.

Miller started back, unwilling to believe, because this man, who on occasion had displayed the most uncalculating physical bravery, was now exposing a shocking cowardice. And why? He scarcely seemed to know himself. The words ran one into the other with the guttural accent of terror. It was something to do with Captain's Island. It didn't pay to anchor there at night. He backed this opinion with a flood of testimony-creeping, lying tales. Miller knew it while he tried to shut his ears to them.

He raised his hand to stop this cruel exhibition. He stared into the frightened eyes. For only a moment the wills of. the two men battled, then the stronger, the more intelligent, conquered. Tony's eyes wavered. His guttural voice ceased.

"Tony," Miller said quietly, "with you or without you, if she can be coaxed through the channel, the Dart will anchor in Captain's Inlet tonight. There's the dingy. Take it if you wish and row to Sandport. You can bring it around tomorrow by daylight. I'll have your money ready."

Tony hesitated. After a visible struggle he turned back to the wheel. The engine gathered speed again. The Dart's nose was pointed for the opening.

"And, Tony," Miller added," since you seem inclined to stand by the ship, you must understand that this nonsense cannot be repeated."

Tony didn't answer, yet, knowing him, Miller felt satisfied. But he noticed that the broad shoulders shook a little.

The boat was entering the Snake. Miller raised his eyes. Perhaps it was the waning light-for the sun was setting-or some atmospheric trick, but all at once Captain's Island seemed to have come nearer. The dense mass of its foliage cut into a flaming sky. Stealthy shadows slipped from it across the bent marsh grass. Miller had a fancy that it was reaching out slowly and surely. For what!

The agent's talk of a spell came back to him. Was it the spell of the place already reaching out for him? He felt suddenly cold. He shivered. If it was the spell of the place it had found him, for his customary cheerfulness was finally throttled by a black, heavy depression. He knew, unless the agent had lied, that monstrous things had happened there. Was it possible that Anderson's, letter referred to their fancied, incorporal survivals? The fact that the question persisted troubled him. Unthinkingly, he accepted the challenge of the island. Closing his fist, he raised it against the line of forest. The absurdity of his gesture failed to impress him. He descended to the forward deck. He stepped close to Tony. He tried to speak-naturally.

"Better hurry her, Tony. It mightn't be a bad plan to get settled in Captain's Inlet before dark."

The Darf crept on through the Snake, twisting and turning in the narrow channel between the marshes. Miller, contrary to his usual custom, remained forward with Tony, his eyes fixed on the sombre island, which little by little they approached.

The sun had set quickly, but its flames still smouldered in the west. Aside from the island, caught in the heart of this barbaric afterglow, nothing served to draw the eye except an occasional melancholy clump of Spanish bayonets or palmettos. The only signs of life came from the dwellers of the marsh-the flapping of a heron, disturbed by their passing, or the far-away, mournful cries of unseen birds.

Miller regretted the thickening dusk. All at once the agent's gossip had become comprehensible. Yet he did not speak to Tony. To have done so would have assumed an undesirable quality of sympathy, of confession. He forced himself against his inclination to return to his steamer-chair on the upper deck. As he climbed the ladder he saw the native send a startled glance after him.

At last the boat took a sweeping curve to the east. The Snake widened and straightened, disclosing an unobstructed vista past the northern end of the island, to sand dunes, piled against the gloomy ashes of the sunset.

A swifter current caught them. It appeared to hurry the Dart, resisting, into the jaws of the inlet.

Miller started up. Tony was straining at the wheel. He seemed to be trying to turn the boat over by the marshes opposite the island, but the current was too strong for him, or the engines too inefficient. In spite of all he could do the Dart kept near the land. Leaning against the rail. Miller watched the struggle and its issue with a feeling of helplessness. Almost before he knew, it they were drawn very near-so near that, even in this rapidly waning light, the dark mass defined itself a little for him.

He saw that the bank at that end was higher than he had anticipated. This appearance of height was increased by a heavy growth of cedars, whose tops had been beaten by the prevailing wind from the dunes and the sea into an unbroken, upward slope. Beneath this soft, thick, and green roof the ancient trunks writhed and twisted like a forest setting for some grim, Scandinavian folk tale.

Behind the cedars palmettos thrust their tufted tops in insolent contrast; and here and there one of those gibbet-like pines lifted itself, dignified, isolated, suggestive.

That first close inspection made Miller feel that it was a place of shadows, offering with confident promise shelter for things that would hide, for things that should be hidden. It carried to him, moreover, a definite menace for the disturber of that to which the island had opened its refuge. To land, to penetrate this jungle, would call for more than physical courage; would, in short, demand a moral resolution, which, without warning; he found himself wondering if he possessed.

Suddenly the line was broken. An opening nearly a hundred yards wide had been torn through the dense mass. A small pier stretched from it to the channel, and from the shore the clearing sloped gently upward to a colonial dwelling. The building was indistinct in this fading light, but Miller knew it for the plantation house where Noyer had lived and ruled before the war.

It was painted white. The main portion was two stories high with a sloping attic roof from the centre of which a square cupola arose. High, slender columns supported the roof of a wide verandah. Wings of one story, curved at the ends, stretched from either side.

That houses absorb and retain a personality is scarcely debatable. The passing of these eighty years-the activities and rumoured cruelties of the earlier ones, the silence and desertion of the later-had given to this house an air of weary sorrow which reached Miller almost palpably. A single light in the left hand wing, yellow, glimmering, like a diseased eye, increased this sensation.

He listened intently, but there were no sounds of life from the shore-utter silence until a bird in the jungle cried out raucously, angrily.

They slipped past. The house was gone. The line appeared to be unbroken again. And the agent had said this was more open, less gruesome than the coquina house where Anderson lived.

Miller went down the ladder. He resumed his stand near Tony, and Tony, Miller thought, sent him a glance of comprehension. He cleared his throat a trifle nervously.

"I suppose we can anchor anywhere about here."

Tony pointed ahead. The shore of the island curved to the south. Opposite it the sand dunes swept around in an exact parallel. As they swung into the inlet the flank of the island slowly exposed itself, scarcely more, however, than a black patch; for the night was on them, and the southern end of the island and of the inlet was lost in shadows —

Tony coaxed and manoeuvred until he had brought the Dart close to the dunes, as far from the island as possible. When he was satisfied he dropped the wheel, ran forward, and let the anchor go. There was a splash as the chain rattled through the eye. Before the noise had ceased the boat turned, listing heavily as it went. Miller, surprised, looked over the rail. The tide was running like a mill-race —ugly black water, dashing by like a mill-race, as if to get past Captain's Island and out to the clean, open sea. The boat was quickly .around and straining at her chain, impulsive to follow.

"Get up your riding-light," Miller said.

Tony came back, shaking his head. Miller understood.

"Run it up just the same."

Tony shook his head again, but he went below for the light. He returned after a moment and ran the lantern to the mast head. Then he went forward, stooped, and examined the anchor chain. Evidently he would take every precaution against being dragged to that sinister shore opposite.

"You're careful tonight, Tony."

The native stiffened. For a moment he listened intently.

"What is it?" Miller asked.

Tony pointed. Miller leaned against the rail, peering and listening too. A soft, regular splashing came to him. Before long he saw a row boat slowly emerge from the shadow of the island.

"That you, Andy?" he called.

No answer came, but the boat drew nearer, at last swung under the stem of the Dart.

"Andy!" Miller called again.

"Take this line, Jim."

It was Anderson's voice, but it was none the less unfamiliar-restrained almost to the point of monotony, scarcely audible as though issuing from nearly closed lips.

"light the cabin lamp," Miller said to Tony.

He bent and took the line. When he had made the row boat fast he held out his hand and helped Anderson to the deck. The hand, he noticed, was hard, dry, a little unsteady.

"Andy!" he said. "Welcome!"

Anderson didn't reply immediately.

"Speechless from joy?" Miller laughed after a time.

"Not far from it," Anderson answered. "Thank heavens you're here. When your wire came last night Molly and I had a real old-fashioned celebration with that demonstrative bottle of wine. You haven't forgotten the fetiches of the Rue d'Assass?"

"And Molly?" Miller asked. "She isn't sick?"

"No-all right. Or as right as can be. That wife of mine-Oh, well, you'll see her, Jim, I hope. You got my letter? We were worried it mightn't reach you."

"I tried to wire."

"Then you know what an uncivilised hole we're in."

He stepped back so that the light from the companionway shone upon him. Miller experienced a sense of shock. Instead of the healthy, pleasant face and the satisfied eyes he remembered, he stared at a lean and haggard countenance out of which eyes full of a dull fear looked suspiciously. Clearly Anderson was the victim of some revolutionary trick of life, or else-it was the only alternative-stood on the crumbling edge of nervous breakdown. Miller hesitated to ask the question that would put the meaning of that extraordinary note beyond all doubt.

"Anyway I'm here," he said. "Your letter would have brought me farther than this. But before we grow too serious inspect my floating palace. It's the low comedian of all these waterways. Picked it up at Bigadoon Beach when the doctor sentenced me."

Anderson put his hand on Miller's arm.

"You must think me a friendly ass, but it confesses my state of mind-that I should forget your illness. You seem yourself again."

"I am," Miller answered. " Never felt better. I wanted one fling with you and Molly before going back to the racket."

The momentary flash of the remembered Anderson snapped out. His eyes sought the deck.

"If you stay it won't be the kind of filing you expect."

Again Miller avoided the issue.

"Which will you see first?" he asked, "The smoke-room, the diningroom, or the saloon? They're all one. Step this way. Lightly, please. We have no double bottoms."

As Anderson reached the foot of the ladder his face brightened, but it was with the envy that comes dangerously near offending the tenth commandment.

"What a cheerful time you must have had!" he said. "How Molly would enjoy seeing this!"

The interior of the Dart was, in fact, unexpected after a glance at her graceless and battered hull. Its former owner had possessed taste and an acceptable definition of comfort.

The walls were painted an ivory tint which took its meaning from four soft-toned French prints. The lockers, running the length of either side, were covered with tapestry cushions. A folding mahogany table stood between them. Forward, a door opened into a tiny stateroom, decorated in the same cheerful fashion, and, opposite, beneath the companion ladder, a low sliding panel led to the kitchen and engine-room.

"Yes," Anderson sighed. "You've been comfortable here. You're lucky, Jim."

He turned away.

"Lucky and selfish. You ought to share your good things perpetually."

Miller laughed.

"Maybe," he said carelessly, "you and Molly have found a more compelling incubus for me on Captain's Island."

Anderson's shoulders shook. Miller looked at him, alarmed. But he was laughing —a little hysterically, still it was laughter.

"Since I'm the point of the joke," Miller said, "you ought to let me in it."

"I was only thinking," Anderson answered, "that Captain's Island is a rare place to look for such a comfort as a wife ought to be."

Miller plunged.

"Andy, I'm waiting to hear about this island of yours, and-and that puzzling Letter. First, something to warm you up —"

He raised his voice.

"Tony?"

Anderson glanced up.

"Tony?"

"My general boatworker."

"Get him North?"

"No —a native."

Anderson watched rigidly while Tony thrust his bearded face through the kitchen doorway and took Miller's orders.

"Now, Andy, sit down and raise the veil." But Anderson still stared at the sliding door.

"This man of yours-Tony!"

"Don't be afraid to talk. I'd confide my most particular secrets to him."

Anderson shook his head.

"I wouldn't trust these natives too far."

Anger coloured his face and voice.

"There's one hanging around the island. Did you see his filthy tub as you came in?"

"No. Good and bad the world over, Andy."

"Be sure of him. You must be sure," Anderson insisted with a vibrant earnestness.

"It makes no difference," Miller said. "The door will be closed. Speak low and he won't hear you. What kind of a mess are you and Molly in down here? Why didn't you bring Molly out with you?"

"At this hour! You'll understand if you stay. It's not pleasant on the island after dark. I —I hoped you'd get here earlier. Don't think I'm fanciful, Jim."

Tony entered and placed the tray on the table. Miller motioned to the cigars. Anderson reached out and drew his hand back absent-mindedly.

When Tony had returned to the kitchen and had closed the sliding door Miller lighted his own cigar.

"Now let's have it," he said.

Anderson leaned forward. His attitude was appealing. There was a definite appeal in his eye. It impressed Miller as tragic that such a strong, self-reliant man should assume this pitiful cloak.

CHAPTER III
THE FEAR IN THE COQUINA HOUSE

Anderson found a beginning difficult. When at last he spoke his voice was low and there were uneven pauses between the words.

"I wanted to come right out and explain the situation," he said. "Then, if you choose, you can pull out of here in the morning. Molly and I talked it over when your letter came. It seemed the only fair thing. But it means telling you in cold blood, and I swore to Molly I couldn't do that. I said you'd call me a superstitious idiot or suspect me of sun stroke. In either case you'll have to include Molly in your diagnosis, and you know how sensible she is."

"Yes, and how sensible you've always been," Miller said. "You don't mean to say you've let this lonely hole get on your nerves?"

"I pray that's what it is," Anderson replied eagerly, " —just nerves. That's why we want to use you-as a sort of test. The truth is we're under the spell of this place, and things are happening-unnatural things-things that we can't explain in any believable way."

Miller tried to smile.

"Sounds as though you were haunted."

"And that's what it seems like. I didn't want to say it myself. It isn't pleasant to be laughed at even when the laugh is justified."

For the second time that day Miller promised not to laugh at anything he might be told about Captain's Island. He was conscious, indeed, of a sharp mental struggle before he had subordinated the impressions he had received himself coming through the Snake and into the inlet.

"I agree not to laugh," he said, "but you must understand in the beginning that I can't take any supernatural talk very seriously. I have no manner of belief in such rot."

"After all, Jim," Anderson answered, "that's the way I want you to talk. It's what we need-somebody with a powerful will like yours and a contempt for the uncanny to straighten us out and bring us back to commonsense."

"Why the deuce have you stayed on if you've been so unhappy?" Miller asked.

"Because we can't yield to a superstition we've never acknowledged. We can't go back to the world, convinced of such madness. Molly is more determined than I. We've sworn for our peace of mind the rest of our lives to stay on until every hope of a natural solution is gone. You're just about our last hope."

"This isn't like you," Miller said. "Frankly, Andy, it's folly."

"Our only excuse for such folly," Anderson answered warmly, "is that we're not the only reasonable people to confess it. There's Morgan who lives in the big house. You must have seen it when you came in. He's more your own sort-absolutely balanced, with a strong will. You'll like him, Jim. He's been our only prop. But little by little I've seen his confidence dwindle, and his uncertainty and worry grow. Then there's Bait, a federal judge in Martinsburg. He brought us down here in the first place."

"That's how you found it?"

"Yes. Bait was a friend of Molly's father. When we were going through Martinsburg on our way to Cuba in January he made us stay over for a few days. He has a fast cruising launch. He knew I was an artist, and he thought I'd enjoy seeing this fascinating combination of jungle, water, and sand. It was a brilliant day, and we came down so fast the island seemed only a step — a charmingly isolated suburb of Martinsburg. Jim, the place seemed to grasp me physically, and to demand, since chance had brought me, that I stay and put on canvas its beauty and the mystery that tantalised even at noon. I felt I had found the inspiration for a new note, for the building of a real reputation. And everything favoured the scheme. The coquina house would do. The fact that we would have neighbours in the plantation house settled Molly. We were enthusiastic and happy about it. Then Bait tried to discourage us. He let us see that even he was subject to this-this folly as you call it."

Miller whistled.

"A judge, eh! He ought to get enough that's beyond the ken of man in his own courtroom. What did your judge say?"

"To begin with he told us the amazing history of the island and old Noyer, its original owner."

"That at least has corroboration," Miller said after Anderson had repeated the agent's story.

"But," Anderson continued, "he couldn't define any real objections beyond the island's isolation, its lack of convenient communication, and-of course-we take them so much for granted now-the snakes."

"I've heard they're the chief tenants," Miller said. "They might have been a sound objection to your settling here."

"But we hadn't seen any that day, and we laughed, thinking the judge was trying to stop up some of his other arguments that wouldn't hold water. And it's true. Neither Molly nor I have seen a single snake, but they're there somehow or other-always-in the background. It's the feeling of the place —a feeling of long, slimy snakes, stealthily gliding in a circle from the shadows with unsheathed tongues. Lately we've feared they were growing daring-were getting ready to strike."

He took out his handkerchief and passed it across his face.

"And these other arguments?" Miller asked. "The ones that the judge couldn't define, that wouldn't hold water?"

"Of course he couldn't convince us with his talk of native and negro superstition while the sun glinted on the inlet and bathed the scene of his atrocious yams."

"Atrocious, you say, yet you —"

"They must be," Anderson said. "Sitting here, face to face with you, I can say it. They must be-Superstitions founded on Noyer's revolting cruelty to his black merchandise, on his terrible fits of rage, on the Arab girl who was pampered and murdered in our house. Beyond question the island is avoided, and these stories, rather than the snakes, are responsible. The boy who brought your telegram from Sandport yesterday stumbled in at dusk, in tears. He refused to go back until daylight-lay awake half the night, crying out These beliefs made it necessary from the first for us to bring our own provisions from Sandport-to drive or walk the three miles to the river end of the island, signal for a boat, and row across."

"Pleasant!" Miller said. "What do the servants think of it?"

"Servants! Haven't had one in the house for two months, except Jake. Same way with Morgan. He's managed to keep his man and a cook. That's all."

"Of course Jake would be faithful," Miller said.

"Yes, he's faithful, but with a painful struggle. Sometimes I feel I have no right to make him stay here, loathing and fearing the place as he does."

"As you do, too, Andy," Miller said softly. "Tell me what has made you doubt the judge's yarns were atrocious. What kind of spooks am I to lay? What do you think you've seen?"

"We've seen nothing. If one only could see! It's more subtle than that. It began the moment we moved down. We had found we couldn't get a native servant near the place so we sent North for Mary and Ellen. You know how attached they were to Molly, how long she had had them."

"Yes," Miller replied, "but ignorant women-easily scared by stories."

"They heard no stories," Anderson said. "There was no chance. We met them at the station in Martinsburg and started immediately on Bait's launch which he had loaned us. He had taken our impedimenta down before, so everything was ready for us. Mary and Ellen were enthusiastic when we sailed into the inlet. They had never been South before. They were excited by the experience, and completely satisfied. But when we entered the house its damp, chill air repelled us."

"It would," Miller said. "I'm told the entire island is a jungle. Such places don't get the sun, and, remember, your house had stood in that jungle, uninhabited, for decades."

"Yes," Anderson agreed, "I ascribed a great deal to the climate at first, and maybe it's that, but-after awhile one wonders."

"First, then, the girls became frightened!"

"I don't know-at first. We all fell silent We started fires in every room, but it seemed as though no amount of warmth could cut that charnel house atmosphere. And the day went so quickly! Black night had trapped us before we had time to realise it. I looked at Molly.

"'If the judge could peep in on us now,' I said, 'the laughing wouldn't be all on one side.'

"So we smiled at each other and were more cheerful after that until dinner time. Then Mary, without warning, burst into tears."

"Homesick in a strange house," Miller suggested.

"We couldn't find out what it was. She didn't seem to know herself. Ellen, of course, had to see it. Their enthusiasm and satisfaction were dead.

"They wouldn't go upstairs until we did. We had given them each a room, but they said they preferred to share one. They hung back from saying good night to Molly. This all drove our minds from ourselves. We went to bed talking about it, wondering what the upshot would be.

"A wild scream awakened me in the middle of the night. In such a place it was doubly startling. Molly was already up. I threw on a bathrobe and we hurried to Mary and Ellen. Their light was burning. They lay in bed trembling and clinging to each other.

"They wouldn't talk at first-wouldn't or couldn't. Finally we got it out of them. They had heard something dreadful happening in the next room. Some one, they swore, had been murdered there. They had heard everything, and Mary had screamed. Jim, I know it sounds absurd, but those girls who had never dreamed of the existence of old Noyer or his Arab woman, described in detail such sounds as might have cursed that house seventy or eighty years ago the night of that vicious and unpunished murder.

"We tried to laugh them out of their fancy. We entered the next room —a large, gloomy apartment on the front, probably-if Balt's story is true-the room in which the woman died. Of course there was nothing there, but we couldn't get Mary and Ellen to see for themselves. Nor would they stay upstairs. They dressed, and spent the rest of the night in the diningroom. And when we came down for breakfast they told us what we had feared, —they wouldn't spend another night in that house. They were ready even to pay their own fare home. They hated to leave Molly, they said, but they couldn't help themselves. They were afraid. It was then that I sent for Jake. If Jake didn't owe me so much, if he wasn't so persistent in his gratitude and loyalty, he would have followed them long ago."

"Nightmares! Nightmares!" Miller scoffed.

"Jim," Anderson said slowly, "since then Molly and I have had the same nightmares."

Miller glanced up.

"Possibly imagination after the girls' story."

"No," Anderson answered with conviction. "We have heard-we still hear-sounds that are not imagination-sounds that suggest a monstrous tragedy. And the worst of it is there is no normal explanation-none, none. Jim, I've tried everything to trace these sounds, to account for them. And they're not all. Aside from this recurrent experience the house is-is terrifying. It isn't too strong a word. You remember all that stuff we used to laugh at in the reports of The Psychical Research Society-footsteps in empty rooms, doors opening and closing without explanation? Well, Molly and I don't laugh at it now-but we want to laugh. Jim, make us laugh again."

"Of course. Of course, Andy."

"And always at night," Anderson went on, "there's that gruesome feeling of an intangible and appalling presence. In the dark halls and rooms you know it is there, behind you, but when you turn there is nothing."

He shuddered. He drank some water.

"In an indefinite way the atmosphere of that house is the atmosphere of the entire island. I can't explain that to you. It's something one feels but can't analyse-something you must know and-and loathe yourself before you can understand. As far as I can fix it, it's the feeling of the snakes, of which I spoke, and something besides. It holds a threat of death."

"And the snakes?" Miller asked; "you say they haven't troubled y —?"

"I said we had seen none."

Anderson paused.

"But," he went on after a moment, "the other day we found Molly's big Persian cat in the thicket between the shore and the old slave quarters. It had been struck by a rattlesnake."

"Too inquisitive cat!" Miller said. "You know snakes don't care about having their habits closely questioned by other animals."

Anderson shook his head.

"If you had lived here the last two months as we have, you might feel as we do about it-that it's a sort of warning. You know I said they were growing daring."

"Andy! Andy!" Miller cried. "This won't do."

"That's what Morgan's always saying," Anderson answered, "but in his quiet way he's on tenterhooks himself. He's resisting the impulse to go, too."

"Has he a wife?" Miller asked.

"A daughter," Anderson said slowly.

"Any company for Molly?"

Anderson turned away. He seemed reluctant to reply.

"No," he said finally, "not even for her father. Jim, I wish you'd try to judge that girl for yourself-if you can, if you see her. You can't tell about her. She's queer, elusive, unnatural. She troubles Morgan. Of course it's a subject we can't discuss very well."

"Off her head?"

"Judge her for yourself, Jim, if you can. Frankly she's beyond me."

"Another puzzle! And that's the entire population!"

"Morgan's two brothers from the North have visited him once or twice. They made it almost jolly. But they didn't stay long. Don't blame them."

"And that's all!"

"On the island proper. There's that native of whom I spoke. One shrinks from him instinctively. He's been hanging around ever since we've been here, living in a flat-bottomed oyster boat, anchored near the shore. At night I've thought I've seen him crawling silently around the inlet in his filthy old tub."

"At least he doesn't seem superstitious." Miller put in drily.

"Rather a figure to foster superstition. He seems to symbolise the whole thing."

"That's a curious fancy. What has he to say for himself? You've been aboard his boat of course."

"Scarcely. Morgan tried that once out of bravado. He found no one there-no sign of life. I've attempted time after time to get a word with the man. I've hailed him from the shore. But he pays no attention-either isn't to be seen at all, or else stands on his deck, gaunt and lean and hairy, etched against the sunset. You look at him until you hate him, until you fear him."

"I can try my own hand there," Miller said. "Then that's the total of your neighbours?"

"There's a colony of oystermen working the marsh banks to the north of the island. They live in thickets. They have the appearance of savages. Bait said there's a queer secret organisation among them."

Miller smoked in silence for some moments, while Anderson watched him with an air of suspense. Miller lowered his cigar and leaned forward.

"This girl, Andy?"

"It's hard to say anything more definite about her, and, if you stay, I'd rather you followed my wishes there. Judge her for yourself, Jim. And-and are you going to stay and help us back to mental health?"

"What do you think?" Miller asked a little impatiently. "You mustn't grow too fanciful."

"If's asking a great deal," Anderson said, "because, sane and strong-willed as you are, Jim, it isn't impossible you should feel the taint yourself."

"I'm not afraid of that," Miller laughed. "I'll stay, but not in your house at first. I'll live on the boat here in the inlet where I can keep my eye on that fisherman of yours and get a broad view of the whole island and its mystery. I'll hold myself a little aloof. You see it would be perfectly natural for you to row out and call on a stranger anchoring here and invading your loneliness; natural for you to bring Molly, say tomorrow; natural for me to return your call, and eventually to visit you at the coquina house over night and experience its dreadful thrills. That's the way we'll let it stand, if you please, for the present. I'm a total stranger."

"Do as you think best," Anderson agreed gratefully.

"Then that's settled," Miller said. "Now how about dinner? You'll stay?"

Anderson arose.

"No, Molly and Jake are waiting. I know they're worried, Jim. They won't have any peace until I'm safely back. These woods-we don't like them even by day."

Miller smiled.

"I'll do my best to purify them of everything but snakes. I can't promise about the snakes."

As he led the way up the ladder he heard Tony open the sliding door. Glancing back, he saw the native, fear in his face, waiting to follow.

"There is something here that gets the natives," he whispered to Anderson. "Go home now and sleep, and tell Molly to sleep. We'll straighten things out in no time."

"You'll do it, if it can be done," Anderson said. "If it can be done —"

He grasped the painter and drew his boat forward against the resisting tide. Miller held the line while Anderson stepped in.

Anderson clearly shrank from the short journey back to the coquina house. A sense of discomfort swept Miller. He felt the necessity of strengthening his friend with something reassuring, with something even more definite than reassurance.

"And, Andy," he said, leaning over the rail. "if anything comes up-if you need me at any moment, send Jake, or, if there isn't a chance for that, call from the shore or fire a gun three times. I should hear you."

"Thanks, Jim. I'll remember," Anderson answered.

He pushed his boat from the side of the Dart. The tide caught it and drew it into the black shadows even before he had seated himself and arranged the oars.

Miller remained leaning over the rail, straining his eyes to find the vanished boat. After a moment he tried to penetrate the darkness for a light, for some sign of that other boat, the boat of the fisherman. He could make out nothing. Yet it must lie somewhere over there, harbouring that grim, provocative figure to which Anderson attached such unnatural importance.

As he leaned there he felt troubled, uncertain. It had been a shock to see a man so, exceptionally sane as Anderson suddenly deprived of his healthy outlook on life and death, and struggling in this desperate fashion to regain it.

He told himself he had no slightest fear of the island or its lonely mysteries. That might after all be a satisfactory explanation: —the loneliness, the climate, the clinging mass of native superstition, the brooding over the servants' fancies, the consequent growth of sleeplessness, and, finally, when nerves were raw, this first reminder of the snakes. It was enough to work on the strongest minds.

Miller smiled at Anderson's fear that he might become a victim too. Yet the impression of unhealth the place had carried to him and which he had fought down before Anderson, had returned. He leaned there wondering.

He swung around at a sharp noise. Tony was at the anchor chain again.

"Afraid we'll drag?"

The native pointed to the sky.

Only a few stars gleamed momentarily as heavy clouds scudded southward. For the first time Miller felt the stinging quality of the wind.

"It'll blow hard," he said. "What a night! I'm going below. I'll be hungry by the time you have dinner ready."

He went down the companionway. The other followed him so closely he could feel his warm breath on the back of his neck.

Tony went in the kitchen and started to get dinner. Miller stretched himself on a locker. He arranged the cushions luxuriously behind his head. He took from the shelf a book which he had found fascinating only last night. He lighted his pipe. He tried to fancy himself supremely comfortable and cosy.

Tony came in after a few moments and commenced to set the table. Miller blew great clouds of smoke ceilingward.

"Not so bad down here, Tony!" he said. "Confess, it couldn't look a bit different if we were tied up at the dock in Martinsburg. Well?"

He lowered his book. He glanced up. The pallor that had invaded the native's face at the command to anchor in Captain's Inlet had not retreated. The fear, too, that had burned in his eyes then showed no abatement. It flashed over Miller that there was a resemblance-not physical, but all the more disturbing because it wasn't —between the Anderson who had just come to him with his appeal and the Tony who recently had bent to his command and traversed the Snake. He found himself questioning if a mirror would not have shown an alteration in his own countenance. The thought troubled him. To drive it out he looked around-at the tapestry cushions, at the familiar ivory panelling, at the four French prints. He had lied to Tony. It was not the same. It did not look the same. It did not feel the same.

He reached up and opened the porthole to knock the ashes from his pipe. A vicious gust of wind tore the brass frame from his hand and entered the cabin. The lamp flickered. Beaching over to regain the frame, Miller's eye caught Tony. He had dropped his work. He leaned heavily against the table, his mouth half open, his eyes fixed on the open port.

Quickly Miller realised that the silent native wanted to talk, wanted to tell him something, strained to go back, doubtless, to those unhealthy rumours whose beginnings he had blurted out at the entrance of the Snake.

Miller's irritation flamed into anger. Decidedly, between Anderson and this superstitious fellow, his own poise would be threatened. Ridiculous! He could not be intimidated by the atmosphere of any place, however lonely, however tarnished by creeping lies. He slammed the frame shut and screwed it tight. He swung on Tony.

"What are you staring at now? Get hold of yourself. Make up your mind to one thing; you'll see no ghosts on Captain's Island while you're with me. Hurry dinner."

It was the first time he had used that tone with the man. He wondered at it, but Tony returned to the kitchen, shrugging his shoulders. Miller, however, noticed that a rule was broken. The kitchen door was left wide.

After dinner he went back to the book which he had thought fascinating last night. Now its cleverness had dwindled. It failed to hold him. Tony, whose invariable custom it had been to retire early to his bunk in the kitchen, sat wide-eyed in the doorway. Several times Miller was on the point of commanding him to close the door. In the end he thought better of it. These irritable impulses were foreign to' his personality. They might be looked upon as a manifestation of the place against which he should guard. So when he went to bed, after keeping up his farce of reading for half an hour longer, he tried to throw himself into an attitude of amused comprehension.

"If it will make you feel any better, Tony, I'll leave my door open a crack. Then you won't have all the spooks to yourself."

A sigh answered him. Tony's light went out. The boat was in darkness.

Miller tried to sleep. But, in spite of the season and the closed portholes, a chill, damp air invaded his stateroom. The wind had increased to a gale. It beat furiously against the boat, which rocked in the uneven gusts. The distant pounding of the breakers brought a mournful undertone across the dunes. The stealthy passage of the tide suggested the flight of such creatures as Miller knew must live and torture in Tony's superstitious imagination.

Convinced that he could not sleep, Miller lay brooding over Anderson's story, sympathising under the stress of this night more and more with Anderson and Molly. Towards morning, however, he must have dropped off, for, when he opened his eyes, the low sun was shining through the port. The charnel house atmosphere had been dissipated. The Dart lay on an even keel. Tony was up. The welcome odour of coffee entered the stateroom.

Slipping on his bathrobe. Miller hurried to the deck, jumped overboard, and fought that racing tide until it was on the point of vanquishing him.

When he was dressed Tony brought him his coffee. He sat on deck sipping it, calmly appraising his surroundings, almost gleefully aware of the retreat of last night's fancies.

He could see the fisherman's boat now, anchored a third of a mile away, close to the shore of the island. It was, as Anderson had said, low, filthy, ancient; but its deck was empty, its owner nowhere to be seen.

Miller's eyes followed the tangled shoreline in the hope of glimpsing the coquina house. But the thicket was unbroken as far as two gigantic mounds of white sand which stretched eastward from near the river end of the island and evidently separated the river and the inlet. From the tide Miller knew there must be an opening to the sea somewhere down there. Probably the inlet made a sweep to the east and ran out between the mounds and the dunes. The tradition that buccaneers had used the inlet was perfectly understandable to Miller. Screened from the marshes by the island and from the sea by the dunes, with a heavy fall of tide, it had been an ideal spot for the careening of pirate craft.

The sun was higher now in a clear sky behind the dunes. The white grains and the polished sea shells here and there glinted jewel-like in its rays. On the summits tufts of long, slender grass waved languidly in a light breeze. It was already warm.

Tony came in and took the cup and saucer. He was about to descend when he paused with a long intake of breath. That same pallor came into his face, that same fixed terror into his eyes as he stared across the dunes.

"What are you gaping at now?" Miller asked good-naturedly.

The lips opened. Tony whispered :

"Look! In-in white!"

During that outburst of yesterday there had been, Miller recalled, something about a woman in white, presumably the shade of the Algerian. He smiled.

"Come, Tony! Not by broad daylight. You only make yourself ridiculous."

"Look!" Tony repeated. He pointed.

Miller gazed across the dunes, shading his eyes. There was something there, close to the sea; something white; something that moved —a woman or a girl.

He sprang up. Laughing, he jumped to the lower deck and drew in the dingy.

"There's one ghost I'll lay for you, Tony."

"Don't go," the native begged.

Miller stepped into the boat, pushed off, and with a few strong strokes reached the dunes. He was curious. He reacted to an exciting impulse. Who was this early morning adventurer in white who moved across an empty shore! It might be the girl of whom Anderson had spoken-that " queer" girl about whom he had maintained so puzzling a reserve.

He hurried among the dunes, no longer able to see the figure in white. But he remembered where it had stood, not more than a quarter of a mile away. He crossed rapidly in that direction, pausing only when the advisability of caution impressed him. It would riot do to assume the usual at Captain's Island. It was far from ordinary that the girl should be there at all, clothed in this fashion. He was by no means sure that he would offer her a welcome encounter. She might try to elude him. Yet he had made a boast of the affair to Tony. He wanted to convince Tony and himself that the normal was not altogether foreign to the place. He planned, therefore, to step from the dunes to the beach almost at her elbow, but at the last dune he paused too long, fascinated by what he saw thus at close range.

She was a young girl, not more than twenty, he thought, although at first he couldn't see her face. She was not tall, and she was very slender. As she stood, clothed in a long, clinging robe of soft, white stuff, bending forward to the breeze, gazing across the waves, she might have been a figure, animated and released from a Grecian marble. Her hair, unloosed, was yellow and reached below her waist. The breeze lifted vagrant strands which the sun caught and turned to gold. And when she turned, as though his presence had been communicated to her in some exceptional manner, he saw that she was beautiful with an elfin face.

So they stared at each other for a moment across the sand. His eyes wavered. With a strong effort he forced them back to hers. He was bewildered by her beauty, by her unexpected grace, by her steady regard. The phrases he had formed, his questions, were forgotten. It was as though in that first glance the girl had closed his mind to everything except her physical presence which, after all, seemed scarcely physical. A wild thought sprang against his reason. Tony's whisper! His talk of the woman in white! He would prove that if only to convince Tony. So, sea and sky laughing at him, he stepped forward.

She relaxed her curving pose, moving back until the water was foaming at her feet. Then he saw that her feet were bare.

It had been only a moment, yet he knew he must speak. He succeeded haltingly.

"You'll forgive the curiosity of a Crusoe. My man said you must be a ghost. I'd like —"

He broke off, because his voice mocked him as though he were addressing emptiness.

Her face had shown no change. He was suddenly aware of a barrier between them. The feeling angered him. He held out his hand. He forced himself to move toward her. Like a flash she turned and ran up the beach.

Afterwards, when he reviewed the encounter, he was amazed, worried. He only knew that the voice of custom had been silent, and that he had answered to a new voice which he had not dreamed of questioning. From where had this voice come, and how had it reached him I He tried to tell himself that it was the desire to go back to Tony with his boast fulfilled beyond argument, for otherwise Tony would not have understood, would not have believed. But that was not satisfying. It might have been their isolation on a deserted beach and the challenge of her flight. Or, since it puzzled him most, that feeling of a barrier could have been responsible. At any rate the world narrowed for a few moments to the strip of beach and dunes. It contained only himself and this girl who ran from him as though he had violated a perpetual and prized solitude. He determined to come up with her and dispel her selfish fancy.

"Wait!" he called. "I only want to ask —"

Again that sense of emptiness mocked him. He ran. Although he knew he should be able to catch up with her almost immediately, she gained at first. And against this feeling of a barrier his determination strengthened. He ran stumblingly, his hands held in front of him, a growing stubbornness whipping him on. He went faster. He forgot to call out reassuringly. With a startled glance over her shoulder she turned in and darted among the dunes. He followed, breathing hard, his mind closed.

He saw her across the slope of a dune, not ten feet away. And now the serene expression of her elfin face altered. There was fear in her eyes. He wondered afterwards that he had not spoken to her then. But the barrier was down. Nothing remained but the end which her inexcusable flight had made necessary.

The end came sooner than he had expected. Cat-like, he walked around the dune. She started back. He turned as though he would go the other way to head her off. She stopped, at a loss. Suddenly he swung, and, tinglingly aware of the soft flesh beneath the robe, grasped her arms above the elbows. He laughed nervously. He stared at her wide eyes and at her face from which the colour had fled.

She strained away from him, yet there was no confidence and little strength in her effort. He let her go. Covering her face, she sank back against the slope of the dune, while the sand, whispering, slipped past her. She drew her bare feet beneath her robe. Her hair fell forward, veiling her face and hands.

"How could you do that?" she asked.

Her voice was so low and soft he scarcely heard it. Oddly, the question held no reproach.

He sat down beside her.

"Why did you run?" he asked.

"I—I was frightened."

"That is not the reason," he said conclusively. "You were not frightened at first when you ran up the beach. I saw your face."

She shivered.

"No," she said. "I cannot lie to you."

Then the world rushed back to him. He remembered Tony and the boat a quarter of a mile away, the island, the plantation, Anderson and Molly. How had he ever accomplished this aberrant thing? He dug his fingers in the sand, and watched the grains form minute, beautiful patterns. He scarcely dared look at her. He was appalled, ashamed.

"Really, you shouldn't have run like that," he said apologetically. "You know I'm not an ogre."

She turned. Her fear had gone. As she looked at him, surprised, he realised more than ever that she was very lovely.

"But you-why did you follow me?" she asked.

He considered. He had no convincing answer.

"Perhaps it was because I wanted to alter the bad opinion your flight suggested. Frankly, it was an impulse. I can't say where it came from."

"You should not have followed me," she said gravely.

She arose.

"Now you will let me go."

"Wait!"

He laughed lightly.

"Since you recall my ability to catch you, please don't make me exercise it immediately."

"What do you wish of me?" she asked with a show of anger.

"Please sit down and tell me of yourself. Can you blame me for being curious?"

Her anger died. She laughed back at him. She sat down.

"Since you want so little," she said.

"Then what were you doing on this deserted strip of sand?"

She flushed.

"I often come-to swim. The ocean is better than the inlet for that."

"Better, perhaps, but not as safe. The undertow—"

"It is safe," she cried. "The sea and I are friends."

"There is something elusive about you. It is hard to ask ordinary questions. But where have you come from?" Where do you live!"

Yet he knew, or he thought he knew, when he asked her.

"Must I tell you that, too?"

"It is very important."

"Why?" she asked.

"Can't you guess? I want to see you again."

"No." she said.

"Yes. It is the only possible sequel. And if you make me run after you, you ought to tell me where to run."

She was troubled. She spoke almost inaudibly.

"You must not run after me again."

"Where, then?" he urged.

She hesitated. She pointed across the dunes.

"On Captain's Island?"

"Yes."

"In the plantation house?"

She nodded.

"Then you rowed across the inlet. You didn't see my boat?"

"I rowed across the upper end. If I had seen your boat I would have turned back."

"For once," he laughed, "the Dart's insignificance is triumphant. And your father-he encourages these dangerous excursions?"

"They are not dangerous. I tell you the sea and I are friends. Besides —"

She smiled.

"I think you haven't looked at your watch."

He drew out his watch. It was scarcely half past six.

"But if I don't go quickly I might not be able to come back again."

Miller arose. He helped her up.

"Then of course," he agreed, "the secret must be kept. Only I wish you might stay a little longer. Since you seem inclined to forgive my incomprehensible impulse-my schoolboy pursuit —"

He broke off, a little bewildered.

"There is a good deal I'd like to ask you," he went on. "It has been very unusual."

"Very-unusual," she repeated uncertainly.

He took her hand in farewell.

"At any rate," he said, "I shall see you again."

"Don't see me again," she begged.

"I shall call at the plantation. You will be there! You will see me?"

She would not meet his eyes.

"Don't see me again."

"But why! I wish it very much. Will you see me when I call?"

"I don't know. I don't know." she whispered.

"You will see me," he said, and released her hand.

She ran lightly away from him. Once she glanced back, then she was lost to sight among the dunes.

CHAPTER V
JAKE'S PREMONITION

Hands in his pockets, Miller gazed across the rolling sands. He moved once or twice, seeking a less obstructed view, hoping to see the girl's graceful figure again. At last he filled his pipe and smoked thoughtfully, questioning the whole extraordinary encounter until a sense of its unreality swept him. But this he fought back. It was not what he wished. Granted that his pursuit had been arbitrary and inexplicable even to himself, he desired it to remain a thing accomplished, a corner stone. Yet was it possible he had thrown a command in his last words to her, and, looking into her eyes, had read obedience?

Certainly he had dealt with no ghost, but a ghost, he felt, might have puzzled him less than this "queer" girl of whom Anderson had spoken with such reserve.

Queer, she undoubtedly was, and he was by no means sure that in some obscure way his own queer attitude towards her might not be laid at her door. But he was convinced that he had shot wide of the mark when he had asked Anderson if she was off her head.

He walked back towards the inlet. All at once he realised he had not asked her her name. The last he knew, but it would have been pleasant to have heard her reply, to have known her first name, to have judged whether it fitted her unconformable personality.

Suddenly he laughed. He saw a wet, bedraggled figure skulking among the dunes in his direction.

"Stand up, my valiant Tony," he called. "Your rescue party's superfluous."

Still he appreciated the man's devotion in swimming from the Dart to bring him aid against the unknown. When he padded up, wringing the water from his shirt, Miller tapped his shoulder.

"I assure you, Tony, that ghost is flesh and blood; flesh and —"

The fact needed no iteration. The soft yielding of her arms beneath his grasp had come back to him. The last vestige of unreality fled from the adventure.

He led Tony to the dingy, whistling cheerily. He breakfasted later with a huge appetite. He realised he was glad Captain's Island was what it was rather than what he had fancied it before receiving Anderson's letter.

His happy humour lasted all morning. Had he tried he could not have disguised its cause, for all morning the strange girl, strangely met, lingered in his mind and tantalised. At times he even forgot his set purpose of watching the fisherman's tub, which, at least when his eyes were on it, showed no signs of habitation.

After luncheon he anxiously awaited Molly and Anderson, but it was four o'clock before he saw a row boat put out from shore. Even at that distance he recognised his friends and the man, Jake, at the oars. He stood at the rail until Tony had grasped the painter and helped them to the deck.

Molly's appearance shocked Miller more than Anderson's had done the day before. She was scarcely thirty, and he had always known her as a level-headed, light-hearted woman, unacquainted with life's darker aspects, and determined, as far as possible, to hold them at arm's length. Yet to-day she looked old. There were grey lines in her hair. Her manner was nervous. She appeared too slender for her clothes.

The same constraint that had come to him at his first glimpse of Anderson spoiled his meeting with this other old friend. He tried to throw the feeling off. But Jake, when he spoke to him, added to it. In response to his cheery greeting, Jake whispered:

"Thank God, you're here, Mr. Miller. Make them go away. There's death on the island. You feel it. If we don't leave it's going to find some of us."

Miller couldn't smile in the face of this tragic conviction.

"Don't tell me you're getting old and fanciful, Jake."

He turned away brusquely. He led Anderson and Molly below to display his comforts. But when, with the air of a museum guide, he pointed out the four French prints, Molly sank on one of the tapestry cushions, hid her face, and began to cry. Anderson put his hand on her shoulder, while Miller looked on helplessly, his morning's cheerfulness evaporating.

Anderson cleared his throat.

"I say, Molly—"

She checked her outburst.

"Don't laugh at me, Jim. Wait until you've been in our house-until you've slept there just one night."

"I'll angle for an invitation in a few days."

"That's wiser, I suppose," Anderson said. "But return our call tomorrow."

Molly sighed.

"If we could only have Jim in the house. Some one normal, with a will, and no nerves to speak of."

"We'll let Jim do as he thinks best," Anderson answered.

"Molly," Miller said, "did either Andy or you know you had nerves before you came to Captain's Island? When it hits back at you this way stubbornness is a vice."

"You're the last one to say that," she answered. "You of all people! You would have stayed."

"I have no belief in the supernatural."

"Neither have we," she said. "Or we didn't have-One is sure of nothing here. Wait until you've stayed a few days, then repeat that with conviction."

"I'll try, and remember this is medicine, so you must swallow it like good children —I find the place attractive, cheerful."

"As we did," Anderson said, "when we saw it at first on a bright day like this."

"You forget," Miller replied, "I came in at dusk last night, and it stormed."

"And last night!" Molly cried. "You felt nothing last night? You were satisfied? You were glad to be here?"

Miller stared back without answering. His morning's cheerfulness was completely routed.

"You were not," she said with conviction. "and soon even the sweetest days will be coloured for you like that."

"I wonder," he said softly.

He suggested that they have their tea on deck, but Molly was anxious to remain in the saloon. There, she explained, she saw for the first time in two months no reminders of Captain's Island.

Miller fostered her illusion by leading the conversation to friends in New York, to happy experiences they had shared there.

Afterwards they prepared to leave with a reluctance that touched him.

When they had reached the deck Miller glanced at Tony and Jake forward. He realised immediately his mistake in leaving the two alone together. They sat there, staring at the island. Their faces were pale. When he called sharply Jake arose and stepped into the boat with the air of a somnambulist, while Tony indifferently, almost clumsily, approached the task of loosing the painter.

After Molly had entered the rowboat Miller yielded to his curiosity. He overcame his embarrassment. He drew Anderson to the opposite rail.

"There's some truth," he confessed, "in what Molly said down there. I did experience some discomfort last night during the storm, but of course it was the loneliness, the oppressive atmosphere, this vicious tide."

"I was afraid you might feel it," Anderson answered, " although I'd hoped you'd keep above it."

"Nothing has developed since we talked yesterday!" Miller asked.

"Nothing-the night at the coquina house was more than usually disturbed. That's all."

"Well-diet's see-that girl of whom you spoke-you called her 'queer.' "

Anderson glanced up, interested. Miller lowered his voice to a halting whisper.

"Isn't there something more you can tell me about her?"

"You haven't seen her!" Anderson asked quickly.

Miller couldn't go the whole way. Either a sense of discomfort caused by his attitude towards the girl, or a desire to isolate the knowledge of the adventure to its two protagonists, made him glide over Anderson's question.

"I'm only more curious since I've seen the place. You can't blame me. Such a girl as you describe, wandering about this lonely island! Since you think it best I'll wait and see for myself. But her father-Morgan-he'll run out and do the honours?"

"Of course," Anderson said, " unless that girl —"

"Always that girl!" Miller said irritably. "Why do you make such an enigma of her?"

"Because," Anderson answered simply, "that is what she is-an enigma, a mystery; and, after all, I couldn't tell you much beyond that."

CHAPTER VI
THE SNAKE'S STRIKE

It was clear and still that night. Although he was not entirely free from the oppressive, indefinable sensations of the previous evening, Miller slept better. Tony, on his part, behaved in the same disturbing manner, sitting silent and motionless in the kitchen doorway until Miller went to bed, then extinguishing his lamp with evident reluctance.

The daylight, however, brought Miller's cheerfulness back to him. He was early on deck, scanning the dunes expectantly; but the girl did not come to the beach that morning. Miller was sorry. He grew discontented.

A small gasoline launch rounded the end of the island at eight o'clock. Miller reawakened to a sense of interest as it chugged noisily in the direction of the Dart. It probably held Morgan. By deft questioning he might learn something of the girl's personality from her father. Why not, indeed, say to Morgan: "I met your daughter on the beach yesterday"! But he remembered he shared the secret of those early morning excursions with her. Moreover, his effort with Anderson had convinced him that he could not speak casually of her.

Morgan was a small man, past fifty, with a stout, pleasant face and a ready smile. He stepped aboard, introducing himself easily.

"Please be frank if you don't care to be disturbed. I thought I'd run over and see. I live in the house at the end of the island. My name's Morgan."

"I'm glad you've come," Miller answered warmly. "I hoped some one from that delightful house would."

"I suppose you're cruising up the coast." Morgan said.

"Yes-anchored here night before last. I find it so attractive I'm in no great hurry to go on." Morgan laughed.

"When the impulse comes, think of us and resist it. A boat in the inlet is an event. Yours is the first in three months."

Miller pointed at the apparently deserted fisherman's craft Morgan shrugged his shoulders. A shadow crossed his face.

"No company. A sour native. You see the Andersons and my household are the whole community. Have you met the Andersons!"

"They rowed out yesterday."

"Now that you know us all you must let us see a lot of you."

"I want to," Miller said. "I'm anxious to look at that old place of yours. It must have a history."

"Too much history," Morgan answered drily. " Still it doesn't do to run down one's own possessions-particularly when economy chains one to them. Come when you wish. Naturally, you're never likely to find me far away. "

Morgan remained, chatting, for only a few minutes. Miller pressed him to stay, for the little man amused him with his genial air and a dry humour. Morgan, however, refused, saying he had promised to go to Sandport with Anderson that morning.

As he watched the launch disappear around the bend Miller lost patience with himself. Why had he found it impossible to speak of the girl to her father? That afternoon, at least, he would take himself in hand. He would open a campaign. He would call on the Andersons early, and afterwards return Morgan's call. He had told the girl to see him at the plantation house, and he recalled the shrinking obedience in her eyes. If he did not see her he would throw off this unaccustomed embarrassment. He would force himself to speak of her to Morgan.

As soon as he had lunched he told Tony to row him ashore. They landed a quarter of a mile below the fisherman's tub. He directed Tony to return to the Dart. He said he would hail him when he wished to leave the island. Then he took the path which Anderson had indicated.

Stunted cedars and oaks met in a thick roof overhead, and an undergrowth of scrub palmettos and creeping vines was tangled waist-high between the trunks. The thought of snakes was inevitable. An army of them might have lurked unseen within a foot of where he walked. He stepped carefully, looking at the ground, keeping his ears open.

Before he had gone half a mile the path widened into a small clearing from the rear of which the coquina house rose with grey, uncompromising solidity. The trees cast heavy shadows across its square front, and over the roof of the tiny stable to its left, Miller paused. The agent had been right. This was lonelier, more enclosed than Morgan's place.

Molly had evidently been on the lookout, for she ran eagerly down the verandah steps to meet him.

"Jim! I'm so very glad you've come," she called.

"Where is Andy?" he asked, taking her hand.

"Had to go to Martinsburg," she answered, " —simply had to. An important letter from his brokers. He had to see a lawyer right away and sign some papers. You can imagine how he hated it. If he hadn't known you were coming —"

"But he'll get back on the little boat this afternoon!"

"Unless this business positively chains him. In that case he thought you would change your plans and stay here with Jake and me."

"Of course I'd stay. That would be necessary."

"We'll know a little after six," she said. "Mr. Morgan went as far as Sandport with him to order some things for us both. I've been expecting him to come by."

She laughed uncomfortably.

"You see, Jim, I've been stark alone in this ghastly place since luncheon."

"Jake?" he asked.

"He started for a walk."

"Here! Without company! I gathered yesterday —"

"Jake," she said, "Was trying to ripen an acquaintance with the Morgans' cook. You're right Nothing less compelling would draw him so far afield alone on this island. And it's such a bright day I didn't think I'd mind his going. I urged him to go. A little relaxation —a little something cheering to think about-you don't know what that means to him, Jim. He ought to be back soon."

Miller turned towards the verandah, but Molly seemed to prefer the clearing. She made excuses for lingering there, pointing out the small view of the inlet which Jake had achieved by cutting away a few of the thickest trees, and describing the canvases which Anderson had planned but had been unable to carry through.

"Why, when the axe was working," Miller asked, "didn't you tear out that mass of undergrowth which threatens to swallow the house from the rear?"

"Jake's been afraid to go in," she answered. "He says he knows it's full of snakes. Looks as though it might be, doesn't it? We haven't dared take the responsibility of forcing him to work there against his own judgment."

"Mayn't I see the house?" he asked. "I acknowledge you and Andy have some reason. Its exterior has a frowning, inhospitable air."

She walked slowly to the verandah. She held the screen door open, motioning him to enter.

He stepped into a large, square, windowless hall. Even with the door open it was difficult to see at first, and he was chilled by the same revolting atmosphere that had crept into his stateroom two nights before.

He shivered.

"You ought to keep a light and a fire burning here."

"It's warm enough outside, isn't it! Whole house is like this. We keep the doors and windows wide, but the heat and light appear to prefer the open."

"Sensible elements!" Miller muttered.

The entire building housed this air of chill decay, and, although the rooms were large and comfortably furnished. Miller was restless in all of them. Molly's listening attitude troubled him. He wandered from parlour to library to diningroom, and even to the kitchen. All bore testimony to Molly's devotion and determination. Molly, Miller made up his mind, must be rewarded-No matter what happened he would see her and Anderson through to the recapture of the mental peace for which they were suffering on here.

"Smoke, Jim," Molly whispered when they were back in the hall.

"Why do we whisper?" Miller asked.

"Then you do feel something?" Molly demanded.

He would not listen to his momentary doubt. Pushing the screen door open, he stepped into the sunlight of the clearing. The doubt became nothing.

"Of course not," he said. "What do you think?"

"Then don't," Molly begged. "You mustn't. But you didn't go upstairs. Will you!"

"Not now, "Miller answered. "I don't want to discount my first dreadful night in one of those bedrooms. When I do stay you mustn't fail to entertain me with your choicest spirits. "

"Perhaps there'll be none for you," Molly said wistfully. "That would mean just nerves for Andy and me."

"I'll prove it," he laughed.

He sat down on the verandah and chatted pleasantly until Molly smiled and laughed with him.

Morgan appeared about half past four on his way home from Sandport. Miller hailed him. Molly had just brought out the tea things, and Morgan looked at them longingly.

"May I?"

Molly beckoned.

"A party!" she called.

"That collection of huts," Morgan said as he came up and sat down," seemed such a metropolis I hated to leave it, so I lingered, ordering much more than I really needed. If Mr. Miller stays on I think I'll give a party myself in a day or two."

Miller laughed.

"Then there'll be one on the Dart."

"We'll capture the air of a real winter resort yet," Morgan said.

He picked up the cup of tea which Molly had poured and looked around with an air of contentment.

"If Andy were only back to enjoy this!" Molly sighed. "Did he say anything more?"

"He expected to catch the boat down to Sandport."

"I hope nothing keeps him. You know I'm getting worried. I can't imagine where Jake is. I think he walked over to flirt with your cook."

Morgan's eyes twinkled.

"That," he said, "adds to the air of a true winter resort"

"But it isn't like him," she said uneasily. "He doesn't know about you two. He wouldn't be likely to leave me alone so long."

"Time is no match for amorous skirmishing," Miller said.

Yet, watching Molly, he saw her anxiety grow, needlessly, he thought. When, therefore, Morgan arose after an hour, he asked if he might not accompany him.

"I had promised myself to call on you this afternoon," he explained, "and I will hunt up Jake and hurry him back."

"Company through that piece of woods," Morgan said, "is always a blessing."

Miller turned to Molly.

"If I shouldn't see him I'll report here immediately, if I may."

"If you would —" she said, relieved.

He joined Morgan at the foot of the steps. They crossed the clearing and walked down the path to the shore where he had landed.

"I'm glad I've a guide," Miller said.

Morgan laughed.

"I'm glad to have some one to guide. Wait until you've seen the path from the shore to the quarters. It would make a Stanley long for Darkest Africa."

"I've noticed," Miller said with a smile, "that you dwellers in this place answer to its loneliness surprisingly."

"I've prided myself on my resistance," Morgan answered, "but the Andersons and I have had a long winter of it. I—I think the place has gotten a little on our nerves. Don't you judge any of us too harshly, young man, until you've been here a reasonable length of time yourself. Then, perhaps, you'll get our standpoint. For instance, while I'm not the least superstitious, the path we are going to take from the shore to the old quarters has an unpleasant effect on us all. It comes down to this : We prefer to walk it by day. Why? I don't know. I can only repeat that I have no belief in the abnormal."

They had reached the shore. Morgan pointed to an opening in the jungle.

"There's the path. Maybe you'll see what I mean."

Immediately they had entered the forest, Miller did, indeed, see. He understood, too, after a moment, why the agent had failed to reach the quarters. The trees and underbrush were so thick that he had an impression of walking in a low, narrow tunnel. He had another fancy that the sharp palmetto scrub along the edges was a warning *chevaux de frise* before a citadel impossible of assault.

It was necessary to go in single file, so Morgan stepped ahead. He no longer spoke, and, in the half light of that thicket, breathing the heavy air of vegetable decay, Miller found his own silence compelled.

They continued for five minutes, during which Miller combatted and tried to analyse this atmosphere, this deadening impulse to silence. He had made up his mind to break the spell, to speak, when Morgan suddenly stopped with a gasping intake of breath.

Miller saw his companion's shoulders grow rigid, saw him slowly turn and reveal a pallid face and startled eyes.

Miller broke the silence now. His own heart was jumping.

"What is it! What did you see!"

Morgan didn't answer, but over his shoulder Miller saw; and he knew that Anderson's fear had been justified, that Jake's prophecy had been fulfilled, for a man's outstretched body was half hidden by the warning *chevaux de frise*. One booted leg lay eloquently across the narrow, ugly path.

CHAPTER VII

THE FOREST VIGIL

Miller had no doubts from the first. He called with a queer catch in his voice :

"Jake!"

But Jake did not answer. The tortured posture cried out the reason.

Miller put his hand unsteadily on Morgan's shoulder.

"Go ahead," he said hoarsely. "Let's see. Let's do —"

"Do" Morgan echoed. "There's nothing to do. He's dead. Here —"

His voice broke off. He stepped forward haltingly. They reached the body and stared down at it with eyes that sought hope hopelessly.

There was no doubt as to the cause of death. The left trouser leg was drawn up. Two holes showed above the ankle. It was easy to reconstruct the tragedy.

Jake had heard enough about rattlesnakes since he had been on Captain's Island to snatch at his only chance. So, instead of attempting to run to the coquina house or the plantation, he had evidently sat down in this jungle which had so justly terrified him and done his best to fasten a tourniquet above the wound. His torn handkerchief and a broken stick showed how hard he had tried. He had never risen again. Perhaps it was too late when his repeated experiments had failed, or, perhaps, his terror had held him prisoner. At any rate there they found him, doubtless within a few feet of where the snake had struck.

Anderson's words of two nights ago when he had spoken of his fancy of the snakes rushed back to Miller.

"Lately we've feared they were growing daring, were getting ready to strike."

And there also came back to Miller Anderson's fear that the death of Molly's pet had been a warning from the snakes.

A snake had struck and death had followed, yet. Miller told himself, there could be no possible connection between that tragedy and the alleged supernatural manifestations which had so torn the nerves of his friends. Morgan's first words, however, reached him with a sense of shock.

"In this path! By heavens, it isn't safe. It was here, just about here, that Mrs. Anderson's cat was struck the other day. We didn't think enough of that. We haven't been careful enough."

Morgan controlled himself with an effort.

"Poor devil! And this will hit the Andersons hard-all of us —"

As he stood, looking down at Jake, Miller thought he noticed something peculiar. He didn't care to appear fanciful, nor did he wish to give Morgan the impression that his own nerves were running away with him. Moreover, he made up his mind he would have plenty of time to convince himself when Jake had been carried to the house. He spoke of that to Morgan.

"Yes, yes," Morgan agreed.

He glanced at his watch.

"I wish Anderson was back. Maybe we'd better wait until then."

"Yes," Miller said, "and is there anything we ought to do-some formality? I don't know much about such things, but it seems to me —"

"By all means. It's a coroner's case," Morgan answered. "We must avoid getting tangled up in any unfamiliar red tape."

Miller nodded.

"We're practically certain to run against a country official who'll probably use all the ceremony possible to impress us with his importance. But what can we do? I suppose Sandport —"

"It's only a collection of fishermen's huts," Morgan answered, "but I believe the coroner for this coast section has his headquarters there. I guess it's best to notify him."

He turned away.

"This is hard to grasp."

"It has to be grasped," Miller said firmly. "It's getting late. What we have to do should be done at once."

"You're right," Morgan answered. "It's the safest scheme. I'll send my man to Sandport to report the case and bring back the coroner. If he hurries they ought to return a little after dark. Then he can authorise the removal. Besides Anderson ought to be back by that time."

"If he only comes!" Miller muttered. "There's a possibility he won't, you know. Anyhow, go ahead. I'll stay here with Jake until the errand's done, until we've satisfied all the pitiful formalities."

He paused. He bit his lip.

"But there's Mrs. Anderson. Confound it! Why isn't Anderson here? She must be told. If neither Jake nor I shows up as I arranged with her, she'll be frantic with anxiety. If you don't mind you'd better tell your man to stop and give her the facts."

"It won't do," Morgan said. "One of us must take that task, unpleasant as it is. I'll try to do it myself. I'll hurry on to the plantation and get my man off, then I'll go to the coquina house and do the best I can."

Morgan started up the path, but after he had taken a few steps he turned back.

"You don't mind staying here? It won't be long."

Miller shook his head, and Morgan went on. The forest closed behind him and hid his hurrying figure.

Miller lighted his pipe, but the smoke seemed to thicken the heavy atmosphere. Instead of soothing it irritated his nerves. After a moment he let the pipe go out. So this was the end of his joyous and determined plans to call at the plantation and force, if possible, another interview with the " queer" girl! He frowned. It seemed that there was always something arising to limit his knowledge of her to that mystifying encounter on the beach.

In a few minutes Morgan appeared with his man. He had evidently explained the situation, for the fellow's face was white and frightened, and he went by almost at a run with averted head.

"I'll be back as soon as I can," Morgan said as he went on to the shore and his disquieting task at the coquina house.

Alone again, Miller settled himself to wait and watch. The light was already failing in that thick vegetation. For some moments he paced up and down, glancing at Jake, dead in this unspeakable way. But that peculiar impression he had received troubled him. He made up his mind, coroner or no coroner, to satisfy himself immediately. He approached the body on tiptoe. He knelt beside it. He leaned over. He even raised one of the wrists to examine the under side. His impression had not been pure fancy. The skin of the wrists appeared to have been bruised. He could detect what might have been abrasions. But it was all very little. As he arose and pondered, the picture Anderson had drawn of the tongue-tied, powerful fisherman, outlined against the coloured sky, came into his mind and lingered. Yet he had not even seen the man himself, and that picture was unquestionably the expression of the hatred Anderson had formed for him. Anyway these slight marks might merely be testimony of some escapade, some accident, several days old; for that matter, mute reminders of Jake's struggles to fasten the tourniquet above the wound. But the feeling of the place crept into Miller's material brain. While the light continued to fail he resumed his pacing.

Morgan was back in half an hour. He was breathing hard as though he had come quickly through the darkening path. He carried Anderson's shot gun. He handed it to Miller.

"I thought it might be some company," he explained, "because I —"

"And Mrs. Anderson?" Miller asked.

Morgan waved his hand in a helpless gesture.

"If her nerves hadn't been in such a state anyway!" he said. "I did the best I could, but it was hard-hard. I offered to stay with her, but she preferred to be alone until her husband came. She said it would only be a few minutes. If he's coming, it will."

"The boat might be late," Miller said.

"We'll hope that's it. You're sure you don't mind waiting here for the coroner, because I ought to be at the plantation. You see —"

He paused. Miller wondered if it was the girl who was calling him back. Morgan cleared his throat and verified his guess.

"My daughter is alone there, except for the cook. I am not in the habit —I suppose I ought to go back."

"Certainly," Miller said. "I'm right as can be here until the others arrive."

"Come for me if you need me," Morgan directed. "And tell the Andersons they'd better run on over and spend the night at the plantation. It won't be very pleasant for them in the coquina house after this. If they've any scruples about leaving tell them to keep my man to help in any way he can. "

Miller thanked him absent-mindedly. Since Morgan had introduced the subject himself, here was an exceptional chance to speak of the girl, to lift, perhaps, the veil from her uncommon and fascinating personality. He crushed down the desire to speak. He couldn't do it under these circumstances. So, reluctantly, he saw Morgan go.

It was nearly dark now. He was glad Morgan had brought the gun. He liked the feel of the sleek barrels as he carried it cradled under his arm.

The dusk deepened. Infernally the minutes lengthened. The night had an oily quality. He could almost feel it slipping down, thickly, chokingly. Pretty soon he couldn't see the path. Jake's body, which had grown dimmer and dimmer, was no longer before his eyes. The branches were so thick that he couldn't be sure the stars were shining. Once or twice he stumbled, and he stood still, not daring to move for fear of leaving the path to flounder helplessly in that thicket whose revolting life had already done for one of them.

He heard rustling sounds increasing about him. He was practically certain that they were leaves whispering in the breeze, yet that feeling of the snakes, of which Anderson had spoken, came to him in all its force. It was easy to fancy these rustling sounds were made by snakes circling him and slowly closing their circle. It was difficult for him to argue reasonably as he stood by black night in the heavy repellent atmosphere of that forest, in a place he knew was avoided for two things : the supernatural and poisonous snakes. Jake's invisible body testified how deservedly. Those sly noises, such as snakes might make, grew everywhere about him. And he was defenceless, to all purposes a blind man, unable to avoid the creeping horror.

He realised now the state of mind into which the island had thrown Anderson and Molly. He held his nerves in leash by a severe effort of the will. He lost all track of time. It seemed to him that midnight must have come and gone before he saw a lantern waving through the jungle.

"Here they are," he thought. "I'm not sorry this is ended."

But it was Molly, bravely strangling her terror, coming through the forest alone.

"Molly!" he called. "What's the matter?"

She started to run. She had almost reached him when he saw her go down. He heard the tinkling of the lantern chimney as it shattered. He put out his hands against the darkness rushing in again. He stumbled towards her. He found her. He got his arms around her and lifted her up. She was half laughing, half crying-laughing hysterically from her accident and her relief at finding him, and crying because of her grief and her fear.

Anderson, she said, must have missed his boat for he had not returned. Morgan's man had come back from Sandport alone. The coroner had refused to follow until morning. He had made no comprehensible excuse. Evidently he shared the general, ignorant fear of Captain's Island. Even duty had failed to drag him there after dark.

Miller groaned.

"Where is Morgan's man?" he asked.

Molly shivered.

"The coroner must have frightened him. Or else he had some experience on the road from the end of the island of which he won't speak. When he got to the coquina house he refused to leave even to return to the plantation. Instead he was sitting cowed and shaking, over a blazing fire he's built in our kitchen. Jim, this is dreadful! I can't realise. Where —?"

But Miller reached out and found her arm. He grasped it.

"No, Molly, that would be foolish. It is dreadful, as you say. But we must face the facts and be sensible. You and Andy must not let this weigh on you. K you can't rise above it you'll have to leave Captain's Island."

"Feeling as we do! We can't."

"Then," he said determinedly, "you can not brood over Jake."

He felt her aim tremble.

"When it's our fault!"

"That's nonsense. Now listen, Molly. You must go right back to the coquina house. It's hard luck you broke the lantern, but you can follow the path."

The muscles of her arm tautened. She drew closer to him.

"And spend the night there alone, except for that frightened man! Jim, anyway, I came with the lantern, but I can't —I can't go through that path alone now, without light. Don't ask it."

Miller was in a quandary. He shrank from the only way out.

"What time is it?" he asked.

"It was nine o'clock when I left the house."

Six or seven hours to daylight! He knew there was no chance of relief from Morgan. When his man failed to return to the plantation he would naturally conclude that everything had been attended to, and that the Andersons had acted on his suggestion and kept him for the night. There was no other course. Miller decided, indefensible as it was, that it would be wiser to leave Jake to the things that prowl by night than to keep Molly during those long hours in that piece of forest. When he proposed it, however, Molly refused even to consider the plan.

"Jake's been faithful to Andy and me for a good many years. If we had let him go back to New York, instead of forcing him to stay here against his will, he would be alive now. No, Jim, we can be faithful to Jake for a few hours no matter what it costs. I'll stay, Jim. I'll watch with you. Don't say anything more."

Miller knew that argument was useless. So they stayed and suffered through the night. More than once Miller was tempted to fire his gun in the hope that Morgan might hear and come to them. It wasn't merely that they could see nothing, that Jake's body lay so near, even that those stealthy noises such as snakes might make caused their flesh to creep. It was something else; something which, Molly said, you felt in that piece of forest more than anywhere else on the island-felt, and loathed, and couldn't analyse.

CHAPTER VIII

THE CORONER FROM SANDPORT

They suffered through those hours because they were together, yet when the dawn came they looked at each other as though they had been strangers. Molly, haggard and shaking, went down the path then on her way to the coquina house. Miller watched on alone in the sickly, early light. He pulled himself together with a struggle. It was easier now to find comfort in logic, to assure himself that his agitation had been caused by the night and the loneliness, aided by the state of mind Molly and Anderson had impressed upon him.

"First thing I know," he said to himself, "they'll have me as much under the spell as they are themselves."

He could smile a little at that thought even now.

The night had chilled him. He paced up and down vigorously while the light strengthened. Here and there a sunbeam broke through and flashed across the foliage. He grew ashamed of his uncomfortable emotions of the dark hours.

It was still early when he saw Morgan walking down the path from the plantation. Morgan stopped, surprised and anxious.

"Why are you still here? The coroner didn't come. And Anderson?"

Miller explained the situation.

"And I stayed at the house and slept peacefully," Morgan said with regret. "Why didn't you run up and get me to help out? I thought when my man didn't return —"

"What was the use of disturbing you?" Miller asked.

"Only," Morgan answered," because two might be better than one for an all night watch here-particularly under the circumstances. Some action ought to be taken against that coroner. It was his business to answer the call."

Miller laughed a little.

"After spending the night alone in this piece of woods I'm not so sure there isn't something to be said in his defence. It's odd how a little loneliness, a little darkness, and the thought of death will make the poise of the strongest of us topple."

"It's this rotten patch of woods," Morgan muttered. "I'm proud of my poise, but I wonder if I would have pulled through such a night as fresh as you."

"Surely," Miller said. "One suffers temporarily, then the reaction comes, and you almost want to try it again to prove what a fool you've been."

But as he spoke Miller knew he did not want to try it again.

"I was on my way to the coquina house," Morgan said. "But you'd better let me relieve you until the others come."

"Thanks," Miller answered. "I suppose I ought to report to my man. He was expecting me on the boat for dinner last night. I've no doubt he thinks the spooks have carried me off and turned me into a spook myself."

He handed Morgan the gun, and went down the path, keeping his eyes open for signs of snakes. That was one element of danger on the island whose existence he was willing to admit

As he stepped from the woods the sight of the Dart filled him with a sense of unreality. It was, however, the very real nature of the picture which gave birth to this not altogether comfortable impression.

He paused on the shore and stared, a little bewildered, while his eyes accustomed themselves to the glamour of an unclouded sun above reflecting water that was glass-like. After the heavy shadows of the forest path it seemed a miracle such light should exist at all.

The Dart appeared to be suspended in the midst of this dazzling spectacle' Beyond her the dunes had the effect of a mirage. The usually mournful and insistent pounding of the breakers had fallen to an indifferent drone.

Miller closed his eyes. What he had seen struck him with a sense of shame after his experience in the forest. For a moment he felt physically ill. He bent his mind to the conquest of his weakness. He recalled Tony. He could fancy the native's frame of mind. After all, he owed Tony the release of that fear. So he opened his eyes again. But there was no one on the deck of the Dart, yet, under the circumstances, he could not imagine Tony waiting below.

He glanced along the beach and saw the dingy. Then Tony, since he had not passed through the forest, must be at the coquina house, unless, indeed, he had yielded to his panic and left the island altogether.

He turned and looked at the fisherman's craft. It floated, filthy and uncared-for. No one was to be seen, nor did its deck disclose any record of recent activity. It lay in the still water like an abandoned hulk. It conveyed the air of tragedy that invariably clings to a wreck when the destroying storm has fled before calm and sunshine. Why, Miller asked himself, should this be so? Why did the fisherman fail persistently to show himself?

As he walked slowly towards the coquina house he completed the conquest of his disagreeable sensations. There would be work to-day requiring a clear head and strength. With Morgan he would have to divide the responsibility of Molly and the dead until Anderson returned.

If only there was some way to communicate with Anderson! Unquestionably he would not return until evening when the little boat would come down to Sandport from Martinsburg. It was another reminder of their isolation, of their helplessness.

When he stepped into the clearing Miller saw Tony and Morgan's man standing in front of the coquina house. The sight of Tony was a tonic for Miller. It helped rout the last of his uneasy thoughts. For Tony's face was white. As Morgan's man talked to him he glanced repeatedly over his shoulder. He raised his hands once or twice. They shook.

Miller accepted it as a matter for pride that the man should have remained on the island in this state of fear without his master's restraining influence.

The other, Miller saw, was in no better case.

His eyes, too, had evidently been strangers to sleep last night. Miller did not need to hear any words. The subject of their conversation was confessed by their faces.

"Well, Tony!" Miller called.

Like a flash Tony turned and ran to him, and Morgan's man sidled forward as if, even by daylight, he craved company in this place.

"You spent the night on the Dart?" Miller asked.

Tony nodded. The gesture in which he spread his arms was eloquent of the torture of those hours when he had been doubtful of Miller's fate.

"Then you know everything," Miller said. "This fellow's told you."

Again Tony nodded.

"I couldn't wait. I came here. I didn't know where else —"

"Your solicitude is pleasing, Tony. You see I'm quite myself still-altogether material."

He glanced at Morgan's man.

"And you passed your entire night here?"

The man looked away.

"Yes," he muttered.

"May I ask why?"

Shame flashed across the fellow's face. His voice was little more than a whisper.

"It's easy to ask," he said.

"Therefore I ask."

The red deepened.

"I had come from the end of the island already, and the path through the woods-it was too dark. It was better to stay there."

He pointed towards the house.

"Although that was empty, and I ain't anxious to try it again."

The flush faded. He spoke with more confidence now. Evidently he felt his plainly confessed terror was justified.

"When you ask like that all I can say is you haven't tried it yourself."

"But," Miller said, "I spent the night in that piece of forest you were afraid to cross. Nothing happened to me. What are you talking about?"

The man shook.

"I don't see how you did it," he whispered. "I don't see how you did it."

Miller laughed shortly.

"Come! That's enough. Tony's growing nervous. You've forgotten the sun's shining now. I must have a little commonsense from both of you. No word of the coroner yet?"

Tony pointed at the house.

"He came five minutes ago," Morgan's man answered. "Inside with Mrs. Anderson."

"Why didn't you tell me?" Miller snapped, annoyed at the delay.

He hurried to the house and entered the damp, unhealthy hall. As the door closed behind him his ugly thoughts of last night rushed back. Without any other provocation than the air one breathed here he could imagine Molly and Anderson hating this house.

A voice came to him from the diningroom. Immediately it aroused a disagreeable sensation. It reached Miller raspingly. Its nasal tone was almost belligerent. A sob from Molly brought it to a pause. Then it continued on the same note.

Miller stepped forward. Molly had evidently heard his entrance, for she met him in the diningroom doorway. Her face was red from weeping. Miller could not be sure her tears had any source beyond the tragedy. He had not caught what the other had said, but he felt if the coroner was responsible in the slightest degree for this breakdown he would like to force that rasping, nasal voice to the humiliating softness of apology.

The coroner followed Molly into the hall. Miller glanced at him.

He was a lanky native, uncouth and with a sharp-jawed, assertive face. His stringy moustache was stained and repulsive. He wore a frock coat which appeared, not unreasonably, as old as himself. In his hand he carried a black felt slouch hat.

As soon as he saw him Miller was glad Morgan and he had decided not to violate any of the formal procedure in such cases.

"Has anything unexpected happened?" he asked Molly.

She shook her head.

"I've just been talking to the coroner, Jim. This is Mr. Miller," she went on, motioning the man forward. "Mr. Miller is a very dear friend of ours —a very old friend. I think he will look after everything as much as possible. As-as I told you I'd rather not be troubled any more than is necessary."

Her voice trailed away.

"That's all right, ma'am," the coroner rasped out. "I've heard your story. Don't see much to be gained by asking you any more now."

"Jim," she said pitifully, "I didn't realise some of the things he's told me."

"Don't think of them, Molly. He's said he's through with you. Trust me for the rest."

"Why are you here?" she asked. "Who-who's with Jake?"

"Morgan. He came along early. He was on his way to you. Of course he didn't know we'd been there all night."

The coroner started.

"You were alone all night back in that patch of woods?" he asked.

Miller nodded.

"If you'll go on out to the clearing," he said, "I'll join you in a moment."

The coroner glanced from one to the other suspiciously. At last he swung on his heel.

"Tell the truth, I'm not against a little sunshine. Say, this house can't be healthy-damp as a graveyard in the springtime."

Molly drew back. She passed her hand across her eyes.

"Go on," Miller said irritably.

The coroner opened the screen door and stepped outside.

"Did he-did he annoy you?" Miller asked. "Was he at all nasty?"

Molly sighed.

"I suppose not. I suppose all he asked and said was necessary. You'd better go with him now, Jim."

"And you?"

"I'm all right alone."

"I wish I could be sure."

"At any rate," she said, "there's nothing else for it at present. Don't keep him waiting, Jim. We don't want him to make it any harder."

"Very well," he said. "I'll leave Tony. He'll be in the clearing within easy call."

She thanked him, motioning him to hurry. So he followed the coroner to the clearing.

Immediately Miller was sorry he had sent the officer ahead, for, his unpleasant voice subdued to an undertone, he was speaking to Tony and Morgan's man, and they listened with increased uncertainty, glancing again over their shoulders. It did not appear to Miller that the coroner questioned them.

"Hello!" he called from the steps. "Shall we be off?"

The coroner turned. He studied Miller, while, with a leisurely air, he took a plug of black tobacco from his pocket, bit off the end, and commenced to chew.

Miller came forward.

"I say, is there any point in delay?"

The coroner continued to stare.

Miller fought down the sense of antagonism the man had aroused. He knew it wouldn't do. Molly had been wise. There was nothing to be gained by encouraging him to mate a difficult task more painful.

He was fair enough to ask himself if this antagonism was justified. After all was it not born of his own disturbed and restless state of mind? On the other hand, what possible excuse did the coroner have for fanning the unintelligent emotions of these two frightened servants?

Miller fought back his exasperation. He put his hand on the other's arm. He softened his voice. He tried to fill it with appeal.

"I mean this is a pretty bad business for us. The man, Jake, had been with the Andersons for years. I'd known him as long as they'd had him. These formalities —I realise they're necessary and all that-but they're dreadfully unhappy for us, so the sooner they're over —I'm sure you understand."

The coroner shifted his weight.

"I'm not holding back. I ain't looking to hang around here any longer than I have to. Say, do you think I'm holding back on my job? Is that what you're trying to tell me?"

"No, no," Miller hastened to assure him.

"Then let's go," the coroner said, and, side by side with Miller, started across the clearing.

"Those two," he commented, "don't seem to be having a mighty pleasant time on this island."

"Yes, they're inclined to be nervous," Miller answered drily.

"Act as though they'd seen something," the coroner said.

He glanced up.

"Understand, I ain't blaming them."

"I suppose you questioned them," Miller said.

"What's the use? Didn't need to ask much. They don't know. Just scared."

After a moment he repeated :

"Don't blame them."

They walked out on the shore. The coroner hesitated before the entrance to the evil path.

"Up there, eh!" he muttered. "Up there!"

He impressed Miller as reluctant to enter the path.

"Mrs. Anderson," the coroner said, "told me you found the body."

"Mr. Morgan and I. We were on our way through the path to the plantation house."

"That lady," the coroner mused, "was quite some upset. Don't seem altogether natural, except —"

He broke off. Miller noticed that a little of the colour had left his uncouth face.

"And where'll we find Mr. Morgan?"

"Up the path with Jake," Miller answered shortly.

The delay here was annoying-it seemed so pointless.

At last the coroner overcame his evident reluctance and stepped into the path. Miller followed him. They walked slowly. The coroner glanced apprehensively to either side as they penetrated deeper into the forest.

"There's one thing," Miller said.

His voice had fallen to the whisper almost commanded by this place.

The coroner failed to encourage him.

"It's been on my mind a good deal," Miller went on. "I was alone with Jake for some time and it was nearly dark, but I noticed something odd about the wrists."

He waited for the coroner to speak, to question. But the other walked on slowly. He glanced with increasing frequency into the impenetrable thicket.

"Something odd about the wrists," Miller repeated. "There were marks-abrasions."

Still the man said nothing.

"I thought it a curious phase," Miller insisted. "What do you think?"

The rasping quality had left the coroner's voice. It reached Miller, low and a trifle choked.

"I don't think until I see."

His back beneath the rusty frock coat shook a little.

"Can't understand why anybody wants to hang out in this hole anyway."

"If you had come last night as we wanted you to —" Miller began.

The other glanced over his shoulder.

"Why didn't you?" Miller asked bluntly.

"When I have to come to a place like this after sundown," the coroner answered, "my job'll be open to somebody else. How much farther is it?"

"Just ahead," Miller answered. "You can see Mr. Morgan now."

Morgan, at the sound of their voices, walked down the path. Miller saw at once that the officer made an unfavourable impression on him, too.

"I'm glad you're here," Morgan said coldly. "If you had come last night you would have spared Mrs. Anderson and Mr. Miller a very serious inconvenience."

Miller motioned Morgan warningly, but the coroner faced him with a touch of anger. The presence of a third person appeared, in a measure, to have restored his self-assertion.

"I've just been telling him," he said roughly, "that no law can haul me to this island after sundown."

Morgan's eyes narrowed.

"What's the matter with this island?" he asked quietly.

"You live on it. Beckon you ought to know better'n me. Go ahead. Who's delaying the procession now?"

Miller shrugged his shoulders. Morgan clearly understood his opinion. Without answering the coroner's impertinence, which had really seemed studied, he turned and led the way up the path to Jake.

The coroner looked about him uneasily. Then he hurried through the formalities, authorising the removal. He arose. His sharp expulsion of breath approximated a sigh. Unconsciously he inserted a comedy touch in the desolate scene by whisking the dust from his frayed and stained trousers.

"That's all we want here," he said.

Miller could not comprehend. He had watched the man. He examined his face carefully now. It disclosed only a pallid uncertainty, perhaps not surprising in the circumstances. Yet he had rushed through the formalities with a haste almost indecorous. Not once had he referred to Miller's definite statement about Jake's wrists.

His eyes wavered before Miller's glance.

"Come on. I want to get out of here," he said.

Miller stepped closer.

"One minute. You've forgotten something."

The man turned disagreeable.

"Not that I know of," he snarled.

"Yes," Miller insisted. "I spoke to you about the marks on Jake's wrists."

"Well? I heard you."

Miller was at a loss.

"I say I heard you," the coroner repeated. "Now let's move out of here."

Miller's impatience momentarily overcame the caution he had impressed upon himself.

"But you haven't said anything," he cried. "A matter as important as that! It might lead to something."

The colour rushed back to the coroner's cheeks. His voice stormed.

"Who do you think you are?"

Miller faced him squarely.

"It is my duty to insist on an examination of the wrists."

"Who says they haven't been examined?" the coroner rasped. "Do I have to account to you for everything I do?"

Morgan laid a restraining hand on Miller's arm.

"That's what I wanted to know," Miller answered; "simply whether you had examined the wrists and were satisfied."

The coroner looked at him curiously.

"See here, young man, are you trying to make a fool of me?"

"One doesn't feel the impulse to humour at a time like this," Miller answered testily. "If I can't get you to take the marks seriously there's no more to be said."

"I didn't see any marks that amounted to anything," the coroner muttered.

Miller examined the wrists again. The abrasions had, in fact, practically disappeared over night. Still he was not satisfied. He turned back to the coroner.

"There are a lot of uncivilised oystermen working the banks to the north of the island," he said. "You know it-or ought to-better than I."

"Who are you," the other burst out, "to say who's civilised and ain't? What's more, if you think you're fitter to run my job than I am, just say so and that's all the good it'll do you."

"Hold on," Morgan put in quietly. "If Mr. Miller is suspicious of any point he is perfectly within his rights to insist upon its thorough investigation."

Miller nodded.

"And do you know, Mr. Coroner," he asked, "anything about the fisherman anchored in the inlet? You must have seen his boat from the shore as we came here."

"Yes, I saw his boat."

"You may not understand," Morgan said. "That fisherman is a very unsatisfactory figure. He has puzzled us a good deal."

The coroner's wrath overflowed its bounds, none too strong. Miller decided, at the best.

"If you want trouble and investigations I can give you plenty of both. I can make it so damned uncomfortable that you'll never get your spunk up again to interfering with an officer of the law that's doing his duty as he sees it Uncivilised! And a poor fisherman can't anchor his boat near your rotten island without getting sneered at by you two. And what's it all about? —some marks on the wrists you thought you seen. What if you did? He probably got them thrashing about in the palmetto. That man died of snake bite. Do you want this permit, or shall I tear it up? I ought to do it."

Miller reached out his hand and took the permit. He had been beaten. There was nothing more he could do with the coroner. Yet the man's explanation of the cause of those marks fell far short of satisfying him. In fact, as he walked down the path, he gazed at the rusty shoulders with a growing uneasiness. He wondered if the coroner hadn't brought into the mystery one more disturbing element.

CHAPTER IX
THE GRAVE IN THE SHADOWS

When they reached the clearing in front of the coquina house, the coroner, who had accomplished the journey in silence, promulgated his last order. Miller guessed it was that which had so affected Molly.

"I forgot to tell you," the coroner said, "the law's clear. The burial must take place by sundown."

"To-day!" Miller cried.

"What day do you think?"

"Wait a minute," Miller said. "I don't believe there's any clergyman in Sandport. Is there?" The coroner snickered.

"We're mostly peaceful fishermen over there. Don't need such things. Now and then on a Sunday night a young preacher drops down from Martinsburg."

"But this isn't Sunday," Miller said.

"If you mean you want one for the ceremony," the coroner answered brutally, "there ain't a chance. You'll have to get along without. Well, so long. I'm glad I'm getting away from this place. Family didn't want me to come at all, but they don't understand the law."

Half way across the clearing he paused and turned, back, calling out. Miller raised his hand in an angry demand for silence, for he knew Molly must hear.

"By sundown, and don't you forget it!"

His lanky form was swallowed by the underbrush bordering the path to the river end of the island.

"What do you think of him?" Miller asked Morgan.

Morgan shook his head.

"Strange," he said, "he didn't care to go into those marks."

"When I first told him of them," Miller answered, "he didn't show the slightest curiosity. You're right. It was strange."

The coroner's mandate added to the difficulty of their situation.

Miller glanced towards the house.

"She's in there. Why in heaven's name did Anderson have to be away at this one time?"

He looked up.

"Of course all Sandport knew he had left yesterday."

"Come," Morgan said "It won't do to grow too fanciful, although I must say the coroner impressed me disagreeably enough. Yet we must remember he was afraid to come last night."

Since there was so little time they agreed on the necessary arrangements. Morgan sent his man to Sandport for the local undertaker. Tony, and the man, when he had come back, dug the grave on the edge of the clearing by the coquina house. There was really little choice-the open spaces on the island were so few. Then remained the difficult task of waiting for Anderson, and-hardest of all-the responsibility for Molly.

At last Miller gathered his courage and entered the house.

"Molly!" he called from the sombre hall.

At first she did not answer and a great fear grasped his throat.

"I say, Molly!" he faltered.

"Yes, Jim," her voice came from the head of the stairs. "Don't worry."

"But up there!" he said. " Isn't it dreadfully depressing up there?"

"Not cheerful, Jim, but would any other place be more so to-day? I know what you've been doing. I want to stay up here."

Perhaps it was best to humour her. Worn out by her night of watching, she might find rest.

Miller walked to the verandah. Morgan and he sat there, talking in low tones. Tony and Morgan's man wandered about the clearing, restless, as if expectant of something unforeseen.

Morgan went home at luncheon time and took his man. Miller had no appetite. Moreover, he felt it his duty to remain where he was. He called Tony to him. During the morning the native had grown momentarily more morose, more nervous. Miller directed him to return to the Dart, get his luncheon, and remain there afterwards until he hailed him.

Morgan was back long before Anderson had put in an appearance. In fact it was late in the afternoon when Anderson walked into the clearing from the direction of Sandport. As soon as he saw him Miller realised they would be spared the pain of announcing the catastrophe.

Anderson knew. His eyes were red. He looked tired. Thoughts of the island and fears that harm might spring there during his absence upon those he loved had clearly held him awake last night.

Miller and Morgan hurried to meet him. They pressed his hand.

"You needn't bother," Anderson said in a colourless voice. "I've heard everything. It's all they're talking about in Sandport. The boy who rowed me across the river couldn't think of anything else. It's horrible-and Molly here alone, unless one of you stayed."

"I was with her." Miller answered.

"I thought you would be. I was afraid. I shouldn't have gone. I didn't want to go. And that one night-the only time I've been away-it had to strike."

He paused. He looked across the water which no longer sparkled.

"Thank God it wasn't Molly," he said softly, "or you, or Morgan. You know it might, have been-very easily. "

"Mr. Miller and I are pretty capable of taking care of ourselves, and of Mrs. Anderson, too," Morgan put in with an attempt at a laugh.

The laugh, however, held no note of conviction, and Miller noticed that Anderson's words had diminished a little the man's ordinarily ruddy colour. He did not wonder at this, for he, too, had reacted uncomfortably to the singsong quality of Anderson's voice, to its unquestioning assurance. Nevertheless he nodded in support of Morgan's reply. No other answer occurred to him.

Anderson straightened his shoulders.

"I must go to Molly," he said. "I scarcely dare think what she's suffered."

He led the way to the house. When they reached the steps Morgan sat down, but Miller, after a moment's hesitation, followed Anderson into the hall.

He did not care to force himself at such a moment on his friend, yet he had said nothing comforting, nothing strengthening. His own temporary weakness reminded him how much comfort and strength Anderson needed.

The character of night had already invaded the hall of the coquina house. Miller spoke with an effort.

"Morgan and I have been talking things over," he said. "We've decided we can t afford to let imagination run away with us. We've gone over the-the accident pretty thoroughly. There's really nothing to stimulate imagination there."

Anderson turned and stared at him questioningly.

"It's horrible," Miller went on. "You know how I feel for you and Molly, but there's nothing out of the way —a simple accident. All those snakes! It might have been expected."

"Yes," Anderson said bitterly, "it might have been expected. The worst of it is, it was. I expected it. So did Jake. It's been in the air. It's the feeling of the place. In the air, Jim! We'd had our warning."

"Don't tell me, Andy, you seriously suspect any connection between the fancies you've had here and this accident."

"I do tell you that," Anderson said fiercely. "As I've said all along, it's the feeling of the place. And you call them fancies! Prove it. That's what we're begging of you, Jim."

"Certainly I'll prove it," Miller said. "The bite of a poisonous snake needs no proof. What can be mysterious in that?"

But, as if in answer to his question, the marks he had noticed on Jake's wrists came back to his mind.

"As a matter of fact," he said, "some abrasions I thought I detected on Jake's wrists offer the only mystery to me."

"What do you mean? What kind of abrasions?" Anderson asked indifferently.

"I can't describe them very well. When I first noticed them it was nearly dark. They were not pronounced. Then this morning they had practically disappeared."

Anderson grew rigid.

"Listen!" he said softly.

There was a stealthy movement at the head of the stairs. For an instant Miller questioned if it was one of the manifestations of the coquina house. Then he remembered how long Molly had waited, how impatient she must have grown.

"It's Molly," he whispered.

Molly's voice came to them. Anderson relaxed;

"Thank heavens you're home. Is that Jim with you?"

"Yes," Anderson said. "I'm coming up, Molly, right away."

They heard her sigh as she went back to her room.

Miller reverted to the puzzle of Jake's wrists.

"Have you," he asked Anderson, "ever seen that coroner at Sandport?"

Anderson started. Miller knew the man's mind had failed to return to the phase he had described.

"What, Jim! Oh! The coroner. Of course he came here."

"Stop listening," Miller said. "It was only Molly before."

"But it's already quite dark in here," Anderson answered. "Soon it will be night. I'm sorry, Jim. What were you saying? You asked something about the coroner."

"Yes. I didn't like the fellow's looks or actions. I asked you if you'd ever seen him."

"This afternoon," Anderson replied. "At the wharf in Sandport —a long, slim man. He spoke to me. He said he was the coroner."

"What else did he say!"

The recollection of the interview appeared to stimulate Anderson. His vague air of a victim facing an irresistible fatality left him. He ceased listening. For the first time since he had entered the clearing, crushed by the news of Jake's death, his voice was colourful, expressive.

"He's a fool —a pompous, cowardly fool. He warned me we had to bury Jake before night It was pretty brutal, coming on top of what I'd just heard. I lost my temper-asked him, since he was so particular, why he didn't run over and see to it himself. Jim, the man turned white. He said there was nothing could haul him back to the island that late in the day-might be dark before he could get across the river again. But he threatened trouble if it wasn't done. Pompous and a coward-like all these natives, except that unholy fisherman!"

"Pompous and a coward!" Miller repeated thoughtfully. "I guess you're right. I couldn't interest him in the wrists, and it made me wonder, but I guess you're right. He was only afraid and in a hurry to get away. Probably that was all. Anyway, stop trying, Andy, to pin. a physical fact to an unhealthy fancy. The spirits didn't get Jake."

Anderson went up stairs, shaking his head. He came down very soon with Molly.

"I can't thank you for what you did last night," Anderson said. "Why-why did I have to be away!"

"You couldn't have done a great deal of good, Andy-except taking care of Molly. There was nothing else any of us could do."

"Taking care of Jake in that piece of woods!" Anderson whispered. "Oh, that was a good deal, Jim —a good deal."

They went outside. There was no longer any excuse for delay. The limit of time appointed by the coroner was at hand. It would soon be dark.

Molly whispered something to Anderson who shook his head.

"I haven't the courage," he said.

She turned to Miller, holding out a pocket prayerbook.

"There's no clergyman," she explained simply. "It's too brutal without something."

Miller cleared his throat.

"I'm scarcely fit, but if no one else will —"

She sighed. She looked at Morgan. She held the book out to him, tentatively, appealingly.

Morgan stepped forward. He took the book, opened it, and fumbled with the pages until he had found the place.

"If it will make you feel better," he said in a low voice.

"Oh, thank you," she whispered.

Morgan walked to the grave over which the gnarled branches of two stunted oak trees drooped. The others gathered near him. The sun was about to set. The coquina house threw a heavy shadow over the little company and across the freshly turned earth and the yawning, expectant pit.

As Morgan commenced to read the sonorous and memorable words the sun disappeared and dusk entered the island greedily.

Miller, who was standing next to Morgan let Ms eyes wander about the gloomy setting for this task which had involved them so unexpectedly. All at once his eyes became stationary. They had shown him something moving on the other side of the clearing, just within the entrance of the path to the shore. It was something white. In this obscure atmosphere it seemed almost immaterial Yet he saw it move almost wholly hidden by the trees.

For the moment Miller's mind was swept from the service which Morgan was reading slowly, almost inaudibly now, for it came to him that the half-seen thing in white, flitting among the trees was the elfin girl.

The reading stopped abruptly. Miller glanced at Morgan. The hand with the prayerbook had dropped. An expression of pain had driven the passive sorrow from Morgan's face as he, too, stared across the murky clearing. At last his eyes went back to the book, and he resumed his reading, but his voice was lower than before and it trembled.

Miller gazed at the forest again. He started. The girl was still there, but she appeared to be off the path and moving through the underbrush which he would have sworn was impenetrable. He told himself that some turn of the path or the failing light created this illusion. In order to convince himself he had to recall the morning on the beach when he had felt the soft flesh of her arms yield beneath his grasp. When he looked again she was gone.

CHAPTER X
THE GRIM FISHERMEN

Afterwards they gathered in the living-room of the coquina house for a moment. Morgan, before leaving, urged Molly and Anderson to return to the plantation with him at least for a few days. They were grateful, but they preferred for the present to remain alone where they were.

"We have to get our bearings again," Anderson explained.

So Morgan left.

"At any rate I'll stay with you tonight." Miller suggested.

"It's better not," Anderson answered. "Molly and I must fight things out."

"That's what Jim said last night," Molly said. "I thought it would be impossible then. "

"It's the turning point," Anderson went on. "If we can't rise above this thing we're beaten. I —I think we can fight this better alone, so for a day or two, Jim-There's no use interfering with your plan of campaign."

Miller nodded. Anderson followed him to the clearing.

"In a day or two," he said as he pressed Miller's hand, "I hope we'll be normal again-as nearly normal as we can be after this. At least I think you'll find us livable, and we can talk to some purpose. Good night"

"Hail me if you want me," Miller said. "I'll look in for just a minute tomorrow afternoon to make sure you're all right."

He hurried to the shore and called for Tony.

It was good to get back to the Bart again and to his lonely meal in her familiar and comfortable cabin. But he found changes on the Dart, too. Tony's face was paler than ever, and his eyes appeared larger and wider. More than Anderson he had the air of facing an elusive but unavoidable fate. Curiously, this complete surrender of the native to abject fear cheered Miller. He found it possible to laugh.

"Forget the spooks and avoid the snakes, Tony, and you'll be all right," he said.

Tony turned away unconvinced. Miller himself, when he had gone to bed and lay listening to the whispers of the tide, recalled those other whispers he had fancied in the forest last night, recalled also the whispered conviction of Jake that death was waiting on the island for them.

At last he slept, and the next morning was so brilliant it was impossible not to respond to it. He scanned the dunes anxiously for the return of the girl who had become for him the real and peremptory mystery of the island. There was no sign. So in the middle of the afternoon he yielded to his overpowering curiosity and directed Tony to row him ashore.

They landed at the same point, a little below the fisherman's anchorage.

"I probably shan't be very long," he said. "It's scarcely worth while for you to row back."

Tony's face clouded. He pushed away and lay on his oars off shore.

Miller went to the coquina house as he had agreed with Anderson. He had intended to remain for only a few moments, but continually they urged him to stay a little longer. The night and the morning had been more difficult than they had anticipated, so he remained with them until, glancing at his watch, he was surprised to find it past five o'clock.

"I'm going over to Morgan," he said, "and tomorrow I'm coming here to spend the night if you will have me. I don't see any use in waiting longer. That broad view I was going to get from the Dart has failed to develop. Everything that has happened has been at close range."

"It's at close range here, Jim," Anderson said. "At close range, yet impossibly far. Come ahead."

Miller found Tony still resting on his oars off shore. He beckoned. Tony, evidently relieved at seeing him again, rowed quickly in.

"I'm going to walk to the plantation, Tony. It may be nearly dark before I get back. Perhaps your temperament would suffer less if you came with me."

Tony shook his head.

"Not in that woods again!"

"Nonsense, Tony. I must. Will you come with me? Or maybe you'd rather rout out that fisherman for company."

He glanced at the filthy tub. During the moment he had had his lack turned the fisherman had come on deck. Miller saw him for the first time. He stood by the rail, outlined against the sky and the yellow dunes. Boots, soiled jeans, and a blue shirt, open at the throat, clothed his great figure. Miller received an impression of steadfast, unreasoning power. For a moment forgetful of Anderson's experience, he put his hand to his mouth and shouted.

"Hal-loo over there!"

The figure remained motionless. The eyes, fixed on the shore line, did not waver.

"Hal-loo!" Miller called again. And again he shouted. He turned angrily to Tony.

"I've half a mind to row out and open his ears. What do you make of him?"

Tony gave it up.

"It's Captain's Island," he said.

"Tomorrow," Miller decided, "we'll try to find out what it is. Now are you coming with me, or do you prefer the neighbourhood of that sphinx?"

Tony glanced longingly at the remote Dart.

"No," Miller said. "I won't be gone long enough to make it worth while. If you went back to the boat it would be a nuisance to get you. Better come with me."

He turned inland. Tony, after a moment's troubled hesitation, followed quickly.

Before entering the forest Miller looked back. The grim figure had not moved. The eyes were still fixed. Miller almost doubted if the man had seen them.

Miller followed the narrow path among the shadows-that tunnel-like path whose first invasion had led to the discovery of Jake's body. He walked rapidly, because in spite of himself he was anxious to get through. Tony followed at his heels, breathing gaspingly.

It was all familiar enough until they came to the disturbed undergrowth where Jake had been found. Miller glanced at the trampled palmettos with a sense of discomfort and increased his pace a little. He began to look anxiously for the first sign of the plantation.

The character of the path did not alter until they saw that first outpost-the jagged, grey wall of a collapsed building. After a few steps there were more of these cheerless ruins, then the outlines of one or two other structures in better preservation. Miller guessed that they were the remains of the old slave quarters.

The path turned between two of the walls into a long avenue, lined with live oaks, which led to the rear of the plantation house.

Miller stepped through, and, breathing more freely, looked around him. The crumbling quarters curved to either side in -a wide semicircle whose ends had been swallowed by the hungry forest. Only two or three of the buildings, which had probably been repaired, possessed roofs.

Miller felt the romantic call of eighty years. He wanted to stop and examine these significant survivals of a unique community-these prisons-these torture chambers, if half that had been handed down about Noyer was true. But he resisted. It would soon be dark. As it was his visit must be hurried. So he told Tony to wait for him in the avenue.

"Perhaps you'll find one of the servants to chat with," he said.

But, as he hurried down the avenue and around the house to the pillared verandah, he saw no servants himself. Morgan opened the door, greeting him warmly. He led him into a comfortable library which occupied the entire left hand wing. High cases with ancient, black-bound volumes circled the room.

Miller glanced at them interestedly.

"Look as though they might have been the original library collected by Noyer," he said.

"I dare say they are," Morgan answered. "It's all old before the war stuff-mostly government reports, dry and valueless. One of my brothers, who is something of a book worm, has run through them. He advised selling the lot by the bale for kindling. By the way I hope you'll stay long enough to meet my brothers. They've immolated themselves once or twice by leaving real winter resorts to visit me. I hope they'll be here over this coming Sunday on their way North. You might enjoy them."

He rang a bell. In a few minutes a man servant entered, bearing a tray with cigars and bottles. Morgan made a good deal of a ceremony of the refreshments. Half an hour or more had passed before he arose to conduct his guest through the house. During that time, as though by mutual consent, neither he nor Miller had mentioned Jake. Evidently everyone on the island agreed with Miller that it was essential the tragedy should not be brooded upon by minds already sufficiently troubled.

Miller found the interior of the plantation house more fascinating than that first view had prophesied. The rooms were low-ceilinged but large. The wood work was rough-hewn. Old-fashioned furniture cluttered the floors. The clothing of the two men was all that brought the mind back from the days of Noyer to the present.

At last Morgan led Miller up a steep ladder to the cupola he had noticed from the water.

Here, in the small, square, unfinished room, Morgan pointed out rusty iron staples driven into the oak beams. Depending from them were wrist and leg irons. Overhead was a row of empty hooks.

"For thongs and lashes," Morgan explained. "It seems Noyer was a disciplinarian. This cheerful apartment was designed for the house servants. In one of the barns there is a far more elaborate outfit, evidently for the field hands."

"Romantic?" Miller said. "Scarcely pleasant, but by Jove, the whole place is romantic."

"And what else you've had a chance to see," Morgan answered quietly. "As I've told you, I pride myself on my resistance, but the island does seem to give out an air. How would you describe it?—Baneful! You've seen how superstition fattens on it. That shouldn't be, but I'm fighting it all the time, not only with my servants. My brothers even, when they're here."

The proper moment had come. Miller caught his breath and plunged boldly.

"And your daughter? Is she superstitious?"

Morgan turned. It was growing dark even in this high room. Miller could not read the other's face-could not be sure it confessed any emotion stronger than surprise.

Morgan spoke with a little difficulty. His voice was hard.

"My daughter! How have you-What do you know of her?"

Miller felt himself placed in the wrong. He was conscious of the hot blood in his cheeks. After all, perhaps, he had been tactless, for Anderson had told him that the girl troubled her father, and he had seen sufficient evidence of that himself.

"The Andersons," he said, "mentioned that you had a daughter."

His choice lay between that and an avowal of his encounter with the girl. He did not care to surrender that memory or her secret. At the moment he found he couldn't.

Morgan started down the ladder.

"My daughter," he said coldly, "is not to be judged ordinarily. She is-peculiar. She keeps a good deal to herself."

They descended to the library in silence. Miller resented the constraint that had arisen between them at the mention of this girl in whom he felt so strong an interest. When he took his leave, however, Morgan resumed his cordial tone.

"It's pretty dark," he said. "I hadn't realised it was so late. You have had experience of that path. Perhaps you wouldn't find it pleasant walking, particularly after your vigil of the other night. Let me run you out in my launch."

Miller laughed a little.

"No. I suppose I should be glad it's dark, so I can go through those woods grinning at the feeling with which they oppressed me the other night. But of course that's nonsense. The path's really all right. Besides my man is waiting for me around the house, and we have the dingy on the shore. I can't inconvenience you and myself for atmosphere."

Morgan laughed back at him.

"After all that's the talk. But mind you don't fancy things in the dark. I want you to come again."

"When you've lunched or dined on the Dart." Miller answered.

"Gladly. How about a lantern?"

"There's one in the dingy. I think I can manage that far."

He started around the house.

"Good night," Morgan called after him.

It was really night in the avenue. Miller walked cautiously to avoid stumbling.

He was disappointed more than he would have thought possible. Primarily he had come to see the girl. She had not appeared. He had misread the fancied obedience in her eyes.

He paused and lighted his pipe. After the match expired it was darker than before. He had not realised it was so late. He smiled at the thought of Tony's terror of the darkness in this place. But where was the man! A slight uneasiness drove the smile away. He called :

"Tony!"

He waited, listening. The night was very still.

His uneasiness increased. Perhaps, though, the native had gone back to the dingy. Yet, Miller felt, he would not have taken that path at dusk alone without some irresistible reason.

He went on. He knew he must be near the end of the avenue, that those dark masses directly ahead were the ruined slave quarters. He wondered why the night was so still. There should be insects, birds, animals, but he heard nothing save the slight scuffling of his feet among dead leaves.

Abruptly he stopped. Miller was not easily startled, yet now his throat tightened. Something was moving ahead —a blacker shadow in the black shadow of a crumbling wall. It stepped out towards him.

"Who's there?" he muttered.

But now he guessed, and he was exultant. She came to him quickly. Her hand was on his arm. He heard her heavy breathing. The girl was frightened. He fought back a quick impulse to put his arms around her, to draw her close. He knew it was unjustifiable. For a moment it was incomprehensible to him. He strangled it.

"I told myself you would see me," he said. "I asked you to see me."

"I have obeyed."

She caught her breath.

"Listen —"

"What is your name?" he asked. "This time you will tell me your name."

"Listen!" she began again.

"Won't you tell me your name?"

She burst out impatiently:

"I have no name for you."

She reached up. She pulled at the lapel of his coat.

"Listen to me —"

Again, as on the beach, a sense of social isolation set him beyond the standards he knew. The logic of reason no longer dovetailed. The impulse grew too strong. His arms were around her. His lips tried to find hers. But he could not find her lips at first.

She spoke hurriedly with an odd catch in her voice.

"This is madness. You cannot do that."

"But I can," he said defiantly.

He drew her head back. He kissed her mouth. Without warning she relaxed.

"You have taken too much," she said in a hard voice. "Now go."

"Yes," he answered, "I shall go, but tomorrow on the beach —"

He released her and walked towards the ruins. He was aware of no shame. Instead a steely triumph filled his heart. He was for the moment a man strange to himself.

He had reached the edge of the underbrush when she caught him and grasped his arm. She was trembling.

"No. Even now you must not go that way. "

"Why?"

"Listen! The night is very still."

"Yes. Why have I done this! Is it love?"

"Don't say that. You must not go this way. Come back."

"I shall go this way."

Her voice rose.

"Not tonight. The woods are not safe tonight."

"Not safe?"

She whispered :

"The throats of the snakes-their fangs are out."

"Wh-what do you mean?"

"I know," she cried. "You shall not go this way tonight?"

Suddenly he stiffened. A choked and horrible cry arose from the path ahead of them-the cry of a man in agony. It seemed to break into a thousand sounds and fill the woods.

She shrank back. Then she recovered and tried to catch at his arm. But he realised. He threw off her hand and plunged blindly down the path. He shouted :

"Tony!"

He heard her faintly.

"Come back! Come back!"

But he stumbled on in the direction of the cry. He could see nothing. He kept to the path by instinct, running, thrusting aside the branches and fronds that reached out to hold him back. At last he heard Tony's gasping breath. The man was just ahead. He was running, too, but slowly, heavily, as one who struggles from the paralysing bonds of fear.

"Tony! It was you! What —"

The man staggered forward. Miller took his arm and hurried him.

"Were you —? Were you —?"

But he scarcely dared finish the question. Perhaps Jake at first had run, too. Perhaps Tony, as he ran, was aware of the pain of two tiny punctures, of the slow mounting of the poison, of the imminence of death on the island he had feared. The weight of his responsibility in urging the man here against his will crushed Miller. He forced the question out.

"Tony! Tony! Were you struck?"

They swayed from the forest to the beach. Far away the riding light of the Bart burned steadily. The peaceful water mirrored the stars.

Miller swung Tony around.

"That place is full of snakes," he said thickly. "Tell me —"

He shook the man.

"Tell me! Tell me!"

Tony did not answer. Miller had a cold fear that he could not. He tightened his grasp.

"What happened? Pull yourself together, man!"

It was a long time before Tony spoke. When he did finally, the words came with difficulty, disjointed, almost unintelligible.

"The avenue-something moved. It was dark-frightened-in the path —I got off—"

"Yes. Yes."

"I don't know. I don't know."

"What happened in the path!"

"Don't know. I couldn't go on." The man's voice rose to a cry. "I couldn't move —"

"Nothing touched you? Nothing held you?" "No. I was alone, and I couldn't move-couldn't see. But I could hear. I heard the rattle."

He paused, gasping for breath.

"I heard it crawling-crawling. It rattled twice."

"But you screamed. How —"

"I don't know. It hurt, but I shouted. I heard you coming. I could move. I ran."

Miller let him go. He walked to the boat and lighted the lantern, trying to tell himself it was stark fear that had held the man captive.

Tony pushed off, stepped in, and took the oars. He rowed unevenly. The boat made slow progress.

Miller raised the lantern to examine the native's face. But his eyes did not reach the face. They were arrested by the knotted hands on the oars. He was unwilling to credit what he saw there. The manner of Jake's death on that same path came back and chilled him. For there were abrasions on Tony's wrists, too, and the man could not tell how they had come there. He was sure of only this : —no one had touched him. He dropped the oars.

"I can't row, Mr. Miller. My wrists hurt."

He thrust his wrists in the salt water. He carried them to his face. He pressed them against his eyes. All at once he commenced to sob, painfully, grossly.

Lowering the lantern. Miller waited for this shocking breakdown to rack itself out. He could not doubt what Tony's wrists had shown him. For the first time he surrendered to a sense of insufficiency and, for the moment, of utter helplessness.

CHAPTER XII
THE CONQUERING INFLUENCE

When they reached the Dart Miller lighted the saloon lamp himself. Sitting on a locker, he directed Tony to come to him and to place his hands, palms up, on the polished mahogany table. Then he leaned forward to examine the wrists more carefully. Immediately he started back with an exclamation. The abrasions were disappearing. Even in this brilliant light he had had to look closely to detect that which fifteen minutes back had struck him like a blow in the uncertain glimmer of a lantern.

He questioned Tony. He went over the entire experience once more, but Tony could tell him nothing further. It was all vague in his mind. The thing that was clearest, that persisted, whose memory still terrified, was the fact that he had stood in the darkness, off the path, unable to move, held apparently by an immaterial but plenary force, while the snake had approached.

When Miller had finished Tony bent his head.

"Now," he asked in that thick voice which always gave the impression of a thing disused, "can't we go from Captain's Island?"

Miller thought for a moment, knowing he would stay, yet striving to be honest with himself. He admitted that he craved cheerful surroundings and experiences ranging within his own comprehension. He did not deny that a feeling of inadequacy to combat the atmosphere of Captain's Island had grown, had tonight assumed disconcerting proportions. But he was aware of no bending of his will. He understood more clearly than ever why Anderson and Molly had stayed on at the coquina house in the face of nervous and physical breakdown. Any other course would have confessed their weakness, would have earned his contempt. He found himself looking forward impatiently to tomorrow night which he would spend there, perhaps in the room where Noyer had committed the murder on which so much of the island's superstition was based. In other words he wanted to bring matters to a focus in order to persuade Molly, Anderson, Tony, and himself that they were the victims of nerves, or of some subtle material fact to which at present no clue appeared. For he would not harbour the possibility of the supernatural's convincing him at the end.

Underneath this healthy, combative instinct, moreover, lay a stronger force which held him to the place-one whose birth and growth and expression troubled him scarcely less than the graver problem. When, yielding incredibly to his impulse, he had held the girl, according to his will and against hers, in his arms; when, her resistance swept aside, he had placed his lips on her elfin ones, he had accepted from Captain's Island a personal problem on whose solution, he realised, his happiness depended precariously. Molly and the others eliminated, he could not leave the inlet now. So he faced Tony with a certain pity, because he understood the man's devotion.

"No, Tony, we can not go from Captain's Island yet. I shall stay until all the cards are on the table,"

Under his breath Tony muttered one word :

"Death!"

"What's that?" Miller demanded sharply.

"Can't fight what you can't see. Captain's Island's full of it. It's always meant death. The other night —"

"Your stories!" Miller said. "All right, Tony. After your experience this evening on top of Jake's death I can't keep you. I can't expect to convince you by laughing at your stories again. In the morning you can go to Sandport, and, understand, I don't blame you. We part amicably."

Tony opened his arms in a gesture of despair. He went back to the kitchen.

"That means, Tony?" Miller called.

An angry rattling of pans came to him. But he knew what it meant. If they got through here with whole skins he would take the fellow North with him.

He slept very little that night. The wearier his brain grew with the puzzle the wider awake it held him. He placed the mystery in the scales with logic and commonsense, but the scales would not balance. The few facts that presented themselves only increased the fantasy of the unknown. From the cases of Jake and Tony an alliance appeared to exist between the island's two radical attributes-its commonly accepted supernatural atmosphere and its poisonous snakes. Both of these unaccountable adventures, one of which had ended fatally, had occurred in the same place-that piece of forest between the shore of the inlet and the ruins. What was the connection between the violent and fatal force that lurked there and the wearing manifestations of the coquina house, and, for that matter, with the oppressive air one breathed after dark at Morgan's —even here on the Dart?

When, for relief from these questions to which no answer would come, he turned to his own problem, the girl, he only found more to trouble, more to mystify. From the first her presence had led him to answer to unexpected and, he felt, inexplicable impulses. And tonight she had come to him with a veiled warning that the piece of woods was unsafe. Had she actually known anything, or was her foreknowledge psychic? For she had given him an impression that that word would fit her better than any he knew. One fact lingered in his memory with triumphant clearness. He did not regret the question he had asked in the black shadows of the ruins. He was eager for the dawn to give him an opportunity to answer it in her presence.

When the dawn came, however, it did not bring its usual release from the fancies of the night. He rose, tired, depressed, irritable. His plunge in the swift waters of the inlet failed to arouse him. As he stood on deck afterwards, scanning the tangled shore of the island distastefully, almost with hatred, that significant sentence Molly had uttered so confidently down there in the saloon came back to him.

"By and by even the sweetest days will be coloured for you like that."

He swung about impatiently. His eyes searched the dunes which were touched with a delicate mauve by the dawn. He felt that the girl would come this morning. Uncomfortable as she was, what had happened last night would trouble her, would bring her to the sands. Moreover, he had told her to come, he remembered, and at the time had not questioned her obedience.

His restlessness increased until he rowed to the dunes. He wandered among them while his certainty fell to a hope, and his hope began to dwindle.

At last he saw her far up the curving beach. She walked slowly. Her head was bowed. She wore a black gown which made her figure seem very slender, rather pitiful.

He hurried to meet her, but, instead of the exultation and the steely triumph of last night, he experienced a growth of his depression until it became sorrow. He wondered if this could be accounted for by her black dress and her downcast eyes.

He took her hand, which she permitted to rest passively in his, and led her to the first dune. There for some moments they sat in silence, their backs against the sand, gazing out to sea where the sun rose in an opal mist. When he spoke his voice was lifeless.

"There is so much to say-so much to ask. I am glad you have come."

She did not meet his eyes.

"You shall not ask me to come again."

"Yes," he answered," because-it is very curious. You would not tell me your first name. I've asked you. I do not know that, but I know I love you."

"Hush!" she whispered. "You must not say that."

"Even," he asked, "if you —"

Now she looked into his eyes.

"Not even then."

"Yet you have come as I asked."

"To tell you that."

"You have told me, and it alters nothing. There is something here-something I can't explain, but it shall not intervene. In the end it shall be as I wish."

"Don't say those things-not even you."

He looked at her dully. Where had his courage and his will of the other morning, of last night, fled? Impatient with himself he burst out :

"What is all this mystery?"

She was a little surprised.

"Mystery?"

"To begin with, about you?"

Her lips tightened.

"There is no mystery about me that you haven't made yourself. Last evening, by the ruined quarters you kissed me against my will."

"It was brutal," he said, "but I am glad, for it made me know that I love you. At least it explains nothing. Yes, there is mystery-mystery about you —"

He turned and for the second time shook his fist towards Captain's Island.

"And mystery there. Perhaps you can lighten it, for it shall be lightened. Last night there was a loathsome, death-dealing puzzle on that island, in that piece of forest. I don't understand it. Tony, who was caught in its mazes, doesn't either."

"Yes," she said, "that piece of woods is often unsafe. If I can help it I shall not go there again, nor must you."

"You see?" he cried. " There is mystery, and you must tell me what you know of it."

"I? Nothing."

"Nothing! Then why do you say it is dangerous! Why did you warn me last night! Why did you call me back! Why did you say that about the snakes-that their fangs were out!"

"Because I knew the path wasn't safe last night."

"And how-how did you know!"

She seemed to be trying to find words that would satisfy him. At last she shook her head, smiling wistfully.

"It is hard to tell you that. I only felt. Since I have been on the island I have felt these things about it. I can't tell you how. I wish I could. I —it's only that while I waited for you in the ruins it came to me that the forest was full of snakes and-and horrors, and that you must not go."

"That explains nothing," he said, disappointed.

She turned away.

"I am sorry. You will think I am-queer."

"Queer!" he repeated. "You want me to believe there is a bond between you and those horrors."

"I did not say that."

"If that is all you can tell me it is absurd."

"It is all I can tell you."

"Remember," he urged, "I love you, and, oh, my dear, you, I think —"

She put her hand in his. He stared at the quick moisture in her eyes.

"I have never known love," she said, "but now, perhaps, you have made me feel that. We must never speak of it again. We must never see each other again."

He drew her to him.

"Never!" he mocked. "You can say that now. There's one mystery I can dissipate. I will speak to your father. I will tell him I love you."

Pushing him back, she sprang to her feet.

"No. You will promise me not to do that."

"Why? It is so natural. Can there be nothing normal here?"

"I have troubled him enough," she said. "He is sweet and kind, and it would trouble him if you should speak of me."

"Why does he dislike one to speak of you?" Miller asked. "Why are you kept so much to yourself!"

"I am not kept," she answered. "I keep myself apart. People make me unhappy. Why must you make me unhappy, too! Why do you torture me with questions I don't know how to answer, that I can't answer! I have told you what I could. Don't ask any more."

"I want to ask you one thing. Did your father come here because of you?"

"No, but he has stayed because of me."

"If you refuse to tell me why," he said, "I shall go to him. I shall ask him, no matter whom it troubles."

"You will end by hating me," she answered, "yet I have done nothing wrong. Perhaps it is better, although —"

She hesitated.

"He could tell you about me no more than I have told you, than you have seen yourself; and I could never come here again in the early morning,"

"But you said-Then you will come after all?"

"When you have gone from Captain's Island." she answered.

He rose and grasped her hands.

"Understand, I shall not leave until I have solved the puzzle of that dangerous forest, of the coquina house-until I can walk the whole ghastly island without the uncertainty and fear of the unknown. Then I shall go, and I shall take you with me."

"No, no," she said harshly, "or, perhaps, you will never leave Captain's Island. I know it. You-even you can't do that. I have told you that I feel these things. It is not safe to fight."

"I shall stay."

She strove for some form of persuasion.

"If my father should leave? He has thought of it. He does not like it. If he should take me away would you give it up and leave with us?"

He smiled

"In that case I think pride would go by the board."

"Then —" she began, and stopped.

The chugging of a gasoline engine reached them from the inlet.

"It is he," she said. "He may go to your boat, for I know he likes you. Hurry back. Don't tell him you have seen me. No one must see me here."

"Except me, and you will come to me here again?" he bargained.

The exhaust of the engine was nearer. She looked wildly around her. Swiftly she stooped and touched her lips to his hand, then she turned and ran up the beach, glancing back at him.

CHAPTER XIII

THE BIVOUAC IN THE MARSHES

Miller walked across the dunes, elated at first by the fugitive caress, but after a moment his depression returned, heavier than before. He had hoped the interview would lead to some solution of Tony's adventure, to the unveiling of the entire affair. Yet all it had brought him on that side was the girl's avowal that she possessed an instinct which warned her when the lurking danger gathered itself menacingly.

He stepped into the dingy and pushed off. Before he had reached the boat Morgan came opposite him.

"Want to fish? " Morgan called. "I'm going to try my luck at the lower end of the inlet."

"Haven't breakfasted," Miller answered, "Bring your boat over."

Morgan stopped his engine, pulled at the tiller, and drifted close. Miller studied him reflectively. Why was it that the pleasant little man surrounded his daughter with such cold reserve? Some unhappy family chapter, perhaps? That would also explain her repeated suggestions that nothing could come of their love. Or was the cause to be traced wholly to the girl herself? At any rate this one subject, as the constraint in the cupola yesterday reminded him, altered Morgan's genial personality completely. Certainly he was good-humoured enough now.

"I see you got back all right last evening. Didn't see any women in white?"

"That's what I wished to speak to you about," Miller answered. "No orthodox ghosts, but something more puzzling."

Morgan was curious. He asked meaningly:

"In that piece of woods?"

Miller nodded, and told him of Tony's experience. As he spoke the good humour faded from Morgan's face. He listened dejectedly.

"What next?" he exclaimed when Miller had finished. "Thank heavens this wasn't another coroner's case. Who'll be the third? See here. Miller, I was really anxious to run you out in my launch last night. I didn't press the point, because I didn't want to appear ridiculous. But I don't feel right about that piece of woods. We've had warning enough now. Even before anything happened, as I told you, the Andersons and I preferred to walk it by day. Now here's the cat bitten there, and Jake, and this unaccountable affair of last night. There's no answer. What in the name of heaven is wrong?"

"I am going to find out what's wrong," Miller answered grimly. "I am going to satisfy myself about that piece of woods before I get through with it."

"You're young. Frankly, I'm afraid of it," Morgan answered.

He sighed.

"If this sort of thing keeps up I suppose sooner or later I'll have to get out. And the plantation seemed just what we wanted. It's lonely enough now. Why don't you come over and spend the night tonight? We can have a game of chess, and I'll promise to get you to bed early."

"I'm sorry," Miller said. "The Andersons have asked me to have dinner and stay with them. Another time."

"I wish you would," Morgan urged.

He laughed uncomfortably.

"Here I am crying for company! Well, one can't always analyse. There is just an unpleasant feeling about the house after dark."

He started his engine and prepared to swing off.

"Sorry you won't try your luck with the fishes."

Miller tried with poor success to make his voice derisive.

"Wraiths are much more tempting game to-day."

"But scarcely as likely to rise to bait, I'm afraid," Morgan answered with a frown.

"Speaking of fish," Miller went on, "reminds me I've yet to call on that fisherman over there."

He turned and gazed at the low hulk, again apparently abandoned. Morgan followed his glance. A troubled look replaced his frown.

"Funny business, that!" he muttered. "What's he here for, and where is he most of the time?"

"I'd like to know," Miller said. "The other day you asked me not to judge any of you too harshly until I'd been at the island a reasonable length of time myself. I'm almost ashamed to suspect that my fitness for judgment at all is decidedly in question. Anderson has spoken to me of a ridiculous fancy. He said that fellow seemed no more real than the atmosphere of the island-in fact, was symbolical of the whole thing."

"Ridiculous, of course," Morgan answered. "Yet I think I understand what Anderson meant"

"I think I can understand, too," Miller said. "That's why I no longer venture to judge."

Morgan expressed Miller's fancy of the other day.

"That boat looks like a wreck —a wreck on which somebody has died hard."

"I've thought of that," Miller replied, "but of course it's all nonsense. There's nothing supernatural anywhere-least of all there. But, I must confess, it startles me to have such thoughts at all; to feel, even subconsciously, the impulse to harbor them. Besides, I've seen the man,"

"Yet, you know," Morgan said, "he isn't often to be seen; and, if Anderson raised the question as to whether anybody had touched him, or heard his voice, or caught him expressing an emotion-Well? What could I say? What could you? You've had your eyes on him. That's all. And how often?"

"Only once," Miller answered, "yesterday when I was starting through the woods to call on you."

"I've been here a long time," Morgan said, "yet I've seen him scarcely more than you. I've called to him. So has Anderson."

Miller thrust his hands in' his pockets.

"I hailed him yesterday. No answer. No move."

"The few times I've had a chance to look at him," Morgan said, "he's been like that."

"Anderson told me you'd been aboard."

"Yes," Morgan answered," rather a foolish expedient to lay that mystery. It amounted to nothing. If there had been anybody watching I'd have appeared a fool."

"Why?"

"I don't know. The puzzle of that wreck, the absence of the man, the lack of any sign of him-it all got on my nerves. I'm afraid I lost my temper."

"One does sometimes experience here a helpless feeling bordering on rage," Miller agreed. "At any rate I'm going to repeat your experiment this afternoon."

"You're going to board him, too?"

"If he doesn't answer when I hail. Maybe he will though. In spite of what I've seen myself and all you and Anderson have told me, I can't conceive of his not either welcoming or resenting my presence in some positive way."

"If he isn't there at all?" Morgan asked.

"No doubt about his being there sometime. And where else, in heaven's name, would he be?"

"Anyway, don't take any chances," Morgan warned.

"I shan't," Miller answered. "Besides, Tony will be with me. You see, Morgan, things have come to a point where it's difficult for me to remain inactive. Tony's affair last night has brought matters to a head, and I feel something ought to be done."

Morgan spread his hands.

"I've said that for a long time, but what to do!"

Miller laughed.

"Perhaps the fisherman can tell me. I'm sorry to have kept you from your sport so long. Maybe the snappers will be all the hungrier. Good luck."

Morgan swung away. As he chugged down the inlet he waved his hand cheerily, but Miller saw that his face was still troubled.

Miller stared after him. The fisherman temporarily left his mind, for Morgan's receding back was a reproach. To be sure he had practically promised the girl not to speak about her to her father, and his reward had been that unexpected and singular caress. Yet, perhaps, it would have been the wiser part to have fulfilled his threat and have had the whole thing out with Morgan. In spite of the man's attitude yesterday Miller could have nerved himself to that course this morning. And, after all, what could Morgan have said! Was an expression of disapproval to be weighed against the possible advantages of such a step? Beyond displeasure, such as he had exposed in the cupola, Miller felt sure Morgan could have offered no obstacles to the interview. He could have convinced the father of his right to demand a frank discussion of the girl and of her apparent elusive alliance with the atmosphere of Captain's Island. Sooner or later that interview must take place, unless, indeed, Miller's boasts were shown to be quite empty and the girl's morbid prophecies were beyond all doubt accomplished.

Miller could not seriously forecast such a state of affairs. If he lived he would marry the girl. Since the very mystery of Captain's Island had hurried him to that conviction, certainly he would not let its manifestations intervene.

As he stared after her father he wondered at his determination. While his love had grown the puzzle of the girl's personality had, instead of diminishing, grown equally with it. She was less tangible, more exceptional than she had been that morning on the beach when the waves had played about her bare feet. "What was this girl that he loved! If it were not for the memory of his blind folly and the one quick caress she had offered of her own will, she would have seemed scarcely more real than the mystery in which apparently she was involved.

Had that caress held a meaning which he had not yet sounded? Had she possibly intended it to convey to him some significant message?

Morgan had disappeared behind the sands at the lower end of the inlet. Miller stirred, shaking his head. Inaction became more and more difficult. There was nothing to draw him to the island until after luncheon, but it occurred to him that he had not yet walked northward through the dunes. It would give him something to do, although he expected nothing in that direction except a glimpse of the marshes where Anderson had said the wild oystermen lived and worked.

"Tony!" he called.

The native came up the ladder and waited by the rail.

"I'm afraid you heard all that Mr. Morgan and I said."

Tony nodded.

"I'm sorry," Miller went on. "You slipped my mind. Still it gives you something to which you can look forward-our call on that fisherman after luncheon. We might not receive a gracious welcome. I fancy, Tony, you wouldn't mind fighting that fellow if he turned nasty, in a way you could thoroughly understand."

Tony's grin was sickly.

Miller sighed.

"And he'd be too large for you alone. I've never been much of a brawler, but, I don't know, Tony, it would be really diverting to fight something here you could get your hands on."

Tony pointed to the end of the island around which they had sailed the night of their arrival

"I said —" he began.

Miller raised his hand.

"Don't begin to crow too soon. Don't misunderstand me. I haven't said the things aren't there, waiting for our hands, because they are if only we can drag them from under cover. They must be. If you ever persuaded me they weren't I'd apply for admittance at the first comfortable lunatic asylum I could find. I'm no nearer believing in your ghosts than I was at first."

Tony's smile showed he was unconvinced.

"At least don't get the jumps over what you heard," Miller said. "I'm going to take the dingy now and row to the dunes. I thought it might be pleasant to wander north along the seashore for a few miles. Do you think I'll meet any spirits in that direction?"

Tony's face was impassive.

"Good!" Miller laughed. "The sands aren't as spooky as the island or you'd warn me back."

He lighted a cigar, descended to the dingy, and prepared to push off.

"A couple of hours at the most," he called.

Tony smiled again.

"Breakfast then?" he asked.

Miller whistled, but he was shame-faced —a little shocked. Breakfast was a meal he customarily awaited with impatience. Tony, of course, had been busy with its preparations while Morgan and he had talked. For the first time he became aware of the appetizing odour of those preparations. He had completely forgotten breakfast. The fact furnished a disquieting illustration of his state of mind. It warned him that Captain's Island was, as Molly had promised, increasing its influence upon him.

He took his cigar from his mouth. It was of large size and heavy quality. Usually that brand served as the last ceremony of his morning meal. He had lighted it absent-mindedly. Only now he appreciated its unfamiliar and harsh taste.

He threw the cigar in the water with a quick gesture. As he stepped back to the deck of the Dart his mind groped for an answer to Tony's comprehending smile.

"Foolish to light that, for your bacon smells good, Tony. After all, I've plenty of time."

He realised its inadequacy. The innuendo would fail with Tony who had had so much experience of his master's appetite.

He went down the ladder and settled himself on the tapestry cushions. As a matter of fact he ate little, for his mind would not release the unpleasant recollection of its slip.

As he walked northward among the dunes afterwards he was more than ever glad he was to spend the night at the coquina house. Before, he had only been anxious to force the fight. Now, to do so impressed him as a necessity.

The dunes, when he had left the familiar section near the Dart's anchorage, lured him on for more than two miles before they altered their character. He threaded his way among the graceful, sparkling mounds, catching, now to the left, a glimpse of the inlet, and, now to the right, the flash of the ocean.

Even here he walked carefully, watching the sand ahead of him. He didn't care to take any unnecessary chances with snakes.

After a long time he scrambled up the side of a high dune and looked around him. He had walked past the curve of the inlet. The end of the island was more than a mile to the south. Across the sands, the marshes, and the water it frowned at him moodily. Even in this warm sunlight it looked forbidding.

He recognised a gleam of white among the trees for the plantation house. The girl was back there long before this. He tried to trace her route to the dunes. Probably she landed over there where the inlet curved and the marshes and the sands were divided by a narrow stream.

He slipped down the shifting flank of the dune and turned towards the marshes. The mounds became smaller and less frequent. Then he passed the last of them. He found that the narrow stream which emptied in the inlet was near at hand. Beyond it the marshes stretched away interminably —a green desert with a few distant clumps of trees which cut into a cloudless sky.

Miller faced straight to the north. There, too, the prospect did not at first vary. As he gazed, however, he thought there was a slight difference. A straight black line against the sky, which he had taken for a dead tree, might be the mast of a boat. Keeping to the sand, he paralleled the course of the stream. Very soon he became convinced that he did, indeed, see a mast ahead.

The marsh straggled now along his side of the stream. It forced him nearer the dunes. As the mast grew sharper and larger and he could see the cords stretched from it, he left the open altogether and sought the shelter of the mounds.

As he had approached unobserved the other morning towards the girl on the beach, so now he crept closer to this boat, apparently secreted among the marshes. He believed he was about to see one of those camps of the oystermen. He remembered Anderson had quoted Bait as saying these men lived in thickets, had the appearance of savages, and were united by some queer, secret organisation.

Miller continued stealthily, answering to a profound curiosity. He could make out now a thicket of stunted cedars and laurel bushes. It hid the boat and the mast for a third of its height.

He chose his path with more care. He tried to keep out of the range of any eyes that might be watching from the thicket at the foot of the mast

The bushes fell away. He paused, examining from behind the shelter of a dune the picture at last uncovered for him.

The dwarf growth twisted from a sandy bank which sloped upwards from the stream and invaded the marsh for a distance of fifteen or twenty feet. Miller guessed that it arranged one of the few shelters offered by the marsh itself for human occupancy.

The boat had been hauled close to the bank. The rough stakes to which it was moored gave the camp a permanent air.

The boat was sloop-rigged. It was squat and, probably, flat-bottomed for traffic in these channels. Unpainted and dirty as it was, it lacked that abandoned appearance of the fisherman's hulk in the inlet.

There was, moreover, life to be observed here. Miller held his breath and studied it.

Three men sat around a smouldering fire on the bank. Bait had been right. They had the semblance of savages. Nor, Miller realised, had he much exaggerated when he had spoken to the coroner of uncivilised oystermen.

The faces of these men were covered with matted hair. It straggled in long wisps from beneath cloths wrapped about their heads in place of hats. Trousers and jackets, torn and stained, clung to their lanky figures. Their sea-boots were the only apparel which appeared to be whole.

Only once while Miller looked did he hear a voice. Now and then one communicated with another by means of a quick gesture, but for the most part they stared from eyes, reddened and narrowed by the wind, into the ashes of the fire. Behind them a rough lean-to, open at the front, and constructed of cedar stakes and palmetto, raised a primitive background. Empty oyster shells and tins littered the bank.

Miller was glad he had approached from the shelter of the dunes. Yet he felt a strong desire to expose himself now, to question these strange men whose habits were, to all appearances, aboriginal. He weighed the question. If he had only brought his revolver he would not have hesitated. It would be scarcely wise, however, to walk unarmed into this gathering since it scarcely lacked the characteristics of an ambush.

He was not blind to the fact that his caution might be an injustice. The appearance of these men, their very moroseness, might be borrowed from an occupation which chained them almost perpetually apart from the basic decencies of life. They might, indeed, welcome him as a diversion from their monotonous and degrading routine.

As Miller hesitated one of them arose and stepped from the bank to the boat. For the first time a voice broke the silence, hitherto disturbed only by the lapping of the water about the stakes and the hull.

"Come," the man said. "High time we was off."

His voice, like Tony's, was harsh as if from disuse, but it was more guttural, more unpleasant, accustomed, one might have said, to a strange language.

The others got to their feet and joined the one on the boat. They raised the sail, cast off the moorings, and, lifting long poles from the deck, pushed their way, with motions timed to odd grunts, northward through the narrow stream.

Miller stared after the oystermen until the marsh grass had hidden everything but the sail which scarcely stirred in the light breeze.

He walked closer then, but the bivouac disclosed no more than it had at first. So he turned and went back through the dunes to the Dart.

What he had seen added materially to his worry. He felt he had made a mistake in urging the girl to return to the sands. It was not safe for her to cross at the upper end of the inlet since these men were so near. She had intimated, however, that the excursion was a common one for her. Perhaps, then, the oystermen never ventured nearer the evil island than their camp. Yet that view would presuppose fear, must definitely remove them as a factor in the situation.

When he had reached the Dart he questioned Tony. The native knew there were a number of oystermen working the banks to the north. Once or twice in the past he had had glimpses of them, but he had never communicated with them intimately. They sold their oysters and what fish they caught, he said, in Sandport.

"They're not a pleasant looking crew," Miller said. "What kind of a reputation have they-for instance among the inhabitants of Sandport?"

Tony showed a little surprise.

"Some," he answered, "have families-friends in Sandport."

"Then you don't think there's anything wrong with these fellows I saw? I must say they looked like pirates."

Tony shook his head.

"Have you ever heard of any secret organisation among them?"

Tony's face was impassive. Miller could not be sure his denial was whole-hearted.

"I don't know."

At least Miller understood he could get no more satisfaction from Tony, He brought a book from the saloon and stretched himself in the steamer chair.

But he could not read. His dejection annoyed him all the more because it was so at variance with his natural character. Yet, try as he might, he could not throw it off.

Morgan went by towards noon, displaying a string of fish.

"Why don't you fish, Tony?" Miller asked. "I expect to spend the night on the island with the Andersons. Since you feel as you do there's no necessity of your coming with me. Row me ashore after luncheon and take the rest of the day and the night to yourself."

Tony shook his head. -His attitude was intensely disapproving, but, through devotion or the fear of being left alone on the Dart, it was clear that he would share the adventure. Miller did not attempt to reason with him now. Tony had too much on his side.

Shortly after luncheon he went down to his stateroom, threw a few things in a bag, and directed Tony to place it in the dingy. He hesitated for a moment, then took a revolver from a drawer, saw that it was loaded, and slipped it in his pocket.

"Row over to the sphinxes temple," he said when Tony had cast off. "You'll agree we can deal with flesh and blood there, and I promised you we'd make him a polite call We owe it to him and to ourselves."

When they were close he hailed the tub, but the fisherman gave no sign. They circled the hull. Its few portholes were covered with dirty sacking so that they could see nothing of the interior.

"Closer!" Miller said resolutely. "I'm going on board."

He climbed over the broken rail. He examined the deck. It was empty. There was only one hatch. Miller faced that. His hand on the revolver in his pocket, he called :

"Hallo, below there!"

Aware of something like the reasonless hatred Anderson had described, he kicked and pounded on the hatch. He called again and again.

"If I were certain he's there I'd break the thing in," he said to Tony. "There's something out of the way here."

He lowered himself to the dingy in a bad temper, and directed Tony to continue to the shore.

"Draw the dingy above high water level, then keep your eye on that boat while I look over the scene of your affair."

Tony shook his head.

"It's day," Miller said. "The snakes are drowsy in sunny places."

He went up the path, carefully examining the underbrush on either side. About half way to the slave quarters, at the spot where Morgan and he had found Jake's body, he saw several freshly broken palmetto fronds. That undoubtedly was where Tony had wandered from the path, where he had been held helpless by some compelling, intangible force while the snake had crept near. But there was nothing else; nothing the whole length of the path to give a clue to the nature of this force, nothing if one excepted the hot, damp air that made breathing almost painful.

In this heavy atmosphere Miller's depression grew. His feeling of helplessness kept pace with it. His nerves jangled. Turning, he harried back to the shore of the inlet.

"Not a thing, not a thing," he said irritably in reply to Tony's questioning look.

He pointed at the fisherman's boat.

"And that fellow —"

Tony shook his head.

The native at his heels, Miller hurried to the coquina house. Anderson and Molly met him at the steps.

"Jim!" Molly called. "What's the matter?"

"Enough," he answered. He told them of Tony's experience.

"And there's something more," he said. "Altogether it's put me out of humour with myself. My nerves seem to be on edge this afternoon."

"You, Jim?" Molly said. "I prayed it wouldn't get you."

Miller made an impatient gesture.

"Nothing has me, but I've ceased blaming you for staying here. One can't be beaten by such madness."

With an effort he forced himself to speak of the girl.

"Andy, there's one thing-that girl."

Anderson's glance questioned him,

"Yes," Miller said, "I've seen her. I want to know all you can tell me about her."

"You don't think she had anything to do with last night? " Molly asked.

"I can't think that."

"She is so strange," Molly sighed.

"I asked you on the Dart, Andy, when you spoke of her as so strange if she was off her head. She is queer, I grant you that-perhaps consciously so. That's a question. Actually she is as sane as you or I. Now what can you tell me about her?"

"Very little," Anderson replied, "that can be put into words. Molly, you —"

"It's so indefinite-the feeling you have about her," Molly said. " We've never seen her much-scarcely at all lately. Occasionally we've spied her running or walking through the forest-always with that curious detached expression on her pretty face. But what to me has seemed hardest to account for is the way she makes you feel when she looks at you out of those big, deep eyes, the way she seems to hold you aloof. But I have never thought she was crazy."

"I'd stake my life she is" Anderson said. "The girl suffers, and I believe it's this island that makes her suffer. Perhaps it affects her even more than it does us. She may be more receptive."

"I've thought of that," Miller answered. "Have you never asked Morgan about her? I tried yesterday and he froze solid."

"He always does," Molly said. "I wanted to be friendly with her, but she wouldn't let me. She made me feel I can't tell you how ill-at-ease. Then she ran away. I spoke to her father. He let me see it made him very unhappy to talk about her."

"But why?" Miller cried.

"Because," Anderson answered, "I think Morgan fears it may be the other thing, or at any rate imagines we suspect it. That would hurt him, anger him,"

"And that's all you can tell me of her!" Miller said. "It's how everything appears in this place-elusive, just out of reach. If we could only get our hands on one fact to start a theory that would hold water!"

"I hate to see you this way, Jim," Molly said gloomily.

"Don't worry. I'll get that fact if it's to be had. Meantime we must deal with something we can't define, something apparently impossible. But we can't sit back in our ignorance and say that and risk its running over us. No matter how preposterous it seems to our commonsense we must take the island at its face value. In the first place, I understand you have to hail a boat every time you go to Sandport. There is no boat at the southern end of the island, opposite Sandport?"

Anderson shook his head.

"There ought to be one," Miller went on. "I'll send Tony to Sandport to hire a rowboat. We can keep it tied on this side."

Molly nodded approvingly, but Anderson wanted reasons..

"This business of Tony's," Miller answered, "has taught me a lesson. I've concluded that stubbornness is a poor relation of discretion. It's brought you nothing but the loss of-well, your peace of mind. It's nearly cost me Tony. I acknowledge nothing except that there appears to have been an incomprehensible and fatal force at large in that piece of forest last night and the night Jake died. Because we haven't been able to get a physical clue to it we can't afford to sit back and say it doesn't exist. It's there. It's dangerous. Suppose it should spread to this house? You haven't been able to get any physical clue to the apparently supernatural manifestations of this house either, have you? Suppose the force should grow stronger and sweep the island? It would come from that direction. You could not get to the Dart, but if you had any warning you might escape to a boat and Sandport."

"It looks like surrender," Anderson said helplessly.

"Nonsense. I'm no more friendly to the supernatural than I was in Martinsburg. We're fighting an unseen enemy,' that's all. We must skirmish against the only line he indicates to us."

He called Tony, gave him some money, and sent him to Sandport to hire the boat. For the sake of the others he forced his depression down. He called out with an attempt at cheerfulness :

"Out of our minds with it! It will be dark soon enough. Andy, bring some kind of a table out here and a pack of cards. We'll try a little three-handed auction, and tonight you'll open that demonstrative bottle of wine-two if we want them. The supernatural's as friendly to cheerfulness as the devil to a clergyman."

"What a blessed change!" Molly said.

"We've done what we could for the present. I repeat I'm not friendly to phantoms. My hands itch to get at their throats."

Anderson brought the table and the cards. It was difficult at first, but finally they grew interested in the game. Before they realised he had had time to complete his errand, Tony was back. He explained briefly that he had hired a good boat, and described its location at the river end of the island.

They resumed their game. It held them until the sun had set, until the dejection that came with the twilight drove their minds from the cards.

"I must think of dinner," Molly sighed, listlessly scoring a hand.

"Tell Tony what to do and look upon it as done," Miller suggested. "Or better yet, why not all of us pitch in and get dinner! It will be good fun. Tony can clean up afterwards while we finish this rubber."

Molly and Anderson agreed uninterestedly.

Tony, who had been sitting on the steps, arose, and, as a matter of course, entered the house with them.

They kept close to each other in the cold, dark interior until Anderson had struck a match and lighted the diningroom lamp.

While Tony made a light in the kitchen Miller brought the lamps from the parlour and the library, and placed them with the one already in the diningroom. They left no shadowed corners there. He called to Molly and Anderson, who were in the kitchen :

"Where's the spirit substantial enough to face this battery of kerosene?"

Tony looked at him disapprovingly. Miller laughed.

"Set the table, Tony, then fill that fireplace as full of wood as you can and set it blazing. Do you mind, Molly, my taking your castle thus by storm?"

"Mind!" she called. "If you had been here every night!"

Miller wandered back to the kitchen. The size of the room made it appear bare, unfurnished in spite of the old-fashioned stove, the iron pump and sink, the table, and the two or three chairs scattered around. There were two windows in the rear wall. One of them was open. Walking over to it. Miller gazed out for a moment, then slammed it shut and locked it.

"I don't see," he said to Anderson, "why you didn't have this brushwood cleared out. It's against this back wall. It's a definite menace. Give me an axe and I'll start on it myself in the morning. If the wind's right we might set fire to it."

He paused.

"For that matter," he resumed thoughtfully, "we might fire that unholy piece of woods."

"Too dry," Anderson said. " There's been no rain here in more than a month. The whole island might go."

"What of it! Small loss!" Miller muttered.

He took off his coat. He rolled up his sleeves.

"Molly, pin an apron on me. I'm to be queen of the kitchen while Andy there does alchemy with bottles. Those chops won't take long. Hurry your magic, Andy."

As she leaned over the stove a little colour came to Molly's face. The sizzling of the meat and the clinking of glass from the table, where Anderson was trying to discount the lack of ice, combined with Miller's constant chatter to raise their spirits.

"It's like a studio feast in the Eue d'Assass," Molly said.

"Remember," Miller said, "the night I came in from Saint Cloud with the new bull pup? We called him Buffalo Bill because his chief aim was the breaking of china and glass."

So they went on, reminiscing almost contentedly until dinner was ready, and they had carried the steaming dishes into the diningroom. Tony spoiled their illusion. He leaned against the mantel, uncomfortably near the fire he had built, staring at the open door to the hall. There was a tortured expression on his face.

"See here, Tony —" Miller began.

But he recalled what the man had suffered last night. He went on more kindly :

"Sit in the kitchen doorway if you wish. Now, Molly, Andy, we'll drink to good health, peaceful minds, and victory,"

The meal went better than they had hoped. They toasted themselves with a semblance of laughter. They drank enthusiastically to the carefree party they would have-if nothing happened-in the most crowded, most brilliant restaurant in New York. Afterwards they arranged the table in front of the fireplace and returned to their game.

After a few hands, however, Anderson looked around.

"May in the South!" he said significantly. "All the windows closed and a blazing fire! Is any one too warm?"

They glanced at each other. Molly shivered.

"Good heavens, Andy!" Miller said with an effort. "I don't know whether the blue ribbon belongs to you or Tony. Morgan's the only man on the island you can talk to without hearing the rustle of spirit wings, and even he's tainted. It's your cut. Deal, Molly."

They played late. Long after the cards had ceased to interest them they went on, cutting, dealing, bidding, making beginner's mistakes.

Tony, on his chair in the kitchen doorway, had fallen asleep. The fire had died down. One of the lamps was out of oil. Its wick spluttered as the flame little by little expired.

Miller glanced at his watch. After eleven! He threw down his cards and arose.

"Molly!" he called sharply. "Keep your eyes from that door. There's no use going on with this farce of cards. Reminds me of one stormy night my nurse filled my infant mind with banshees."

He gripped the back of his chair.

"Children, I'm ready for whatever horrors the coquina house can afford."

While Molly arose reluctantly Anderson remained in his chair, staring at the smouldering logs.

"Jim," Molly pleaded," don't hear anything tonight. Don't let your mind be filled with awful things. If only you could come down in the morning and look us in the eyes and say you had slept well."

"I'll do that," he answered, "or if I'm disturbed I'll disturb back as hard as I can."

Anderson looked up, shaking his head.

"I've tried it. There's nothing we can disturb. Perhaps tonight, though-There are nights when one sleeps peacefully."

"If there weren't," Molly breathed.

"But you can't tell," Anderson went on. "One waits."

"Doubtless a newcomer won't fail of entertainment," Miller said.

He walked over and shook Tony, who sprang to his feet.

"Start your fire again," he suggested, "and draw that sofa over. You'll be all right here. He can keep one of these good lamps, Molly?"

She nodded.

"Then, Andy, please take the other and show me to my room."

Anderson obeyed slowly. With lagging steps he led them to the hall. The hall was cold after the heated diningroom. Anderson started up the steps. Molly followed him. Miller went last, curbing a strong desire to glance over his shoulder. At the landing he did look back. Tony had come to the door, where he stood staring after them hungrily.

The stairs swung back from the landing to a square hallway out of which four doors opened. Anderson walked to the one in the farther right hand corner. He put his hand on the knob, waited a moment, then pushed the door open and stepped in. Molly, grasping his arm, followed him. Miller entered after her.

Anderson set the lamp on a bureau which stood between the two windows in the front wall. While he lighted a sconce of candles there. Miller glanced around the apartment where he was to spend the night in an effort to prove to his friends that the supernatural is wholly subjective and chiefly neurasthenic. As he looked, he felt none too confident. The room was huge and dingy. It had an outworn air, the air of a thing past use, a thing dead and decayed. A massive walnut bed-stead stood beneath a canopy opposite the bureau. There was a fireplace set in the wall to its right. A washstand had been placed to its left, and carved chairs stood on either side at the head of the bed. The wall paper, ancient and stained broadly, had a pattern of tarnished bronze arabesques on a green background. Miller fancied it gave out an odour, acrid and unhealthy. In two or three places it had fallen away from the ceiling moulding and hung in pallid tatters. The room chilled him-He turned to the others. Molly had her hand on her husband's arm. Anderson, ready to go, had taken up the lamp. The lamp shook.

"At least," Miller said, "the summer heat can't be blamed for the state of one's nerves on Captain's Island."

He glanced around, again.

"Once this must have been very comfortable-for its period, even luxurious. Evidently Noyer humoured the fair lady. I assume you've honoured me. This is the room in which he cut her throat?"

"I don't know," Anderson said. "This is the largest room. It is a little harder to sleep here. It's where the girls said they heard —"

"Jim, I begged Andy not to. There's a smaller room in the back if you'd rather."

"I choose to sleep here and remember I'm grown up," Miller laughed.

His laughter stopped abruptly. In that room it had a hollow sound. It startled them all.

"You see!" Molly said.

Miller tried to hide his own shock.

"Merely disuse," he answered. "The room is unaccustomed to good spirits."

He laughed again challengingly.

"Tomorrow I'll show you how to get rid of the bad ones. I'll build a fire here and smoke them out. If that doesn't work I'll send up to Martinsburg for a vacuum cleaner. From the advertisements the tiniest, most immaterial wraith wouldn't have a ghost of a chance."

"No, Jim," Molly whispered. "Don't."

She had assumed that air of strained expectancy. Leaning a little forward, her head to one side, she listened.

Anderson touched her timidly.

"Come, Molly. Let's give Jim an opportunity to put his will on the firing line."

"It's been there all along." Miller answered.

Molly turned at the threshold.

"We're just opposite. We'll leave our door open a crack."

"Mine, too," Miller said. "It's a custom Tony's foisted upon me on the Dart! Good night, and go to sleep. Let them perform exclusively for me this once."

As their steps died away across the wide hall the smile Miller had forced to his lips vanished. He turned slowly and, alone, faced the decayed room, again conscious of that disagreeable odour that seemed to come from the wall paper.

CHAPTER XVI
THE CRY IN THE NIGHT

One thing admitted no question. This cold was unnatural unless the state of one's mind could affect the body so materially.

He strode to one of the windows. He flung it open. Leaning across the sill, he took deep breaths of the outside air. That, too, was cold, and a biting wind stole down from the north.

He drew his coat tighter. He tried to realise that a few hours ago he had perspired and gasped for breath in the dangerous forest. He looked at the sullen sky. A dim and formless moon was suspended above the dunes. It showed him a tiny patch of the inlet, but the water did not sparkle. From far across the inlet and the sands came the muffed pounding of the breakers.

Shivering, he faced the room again. The tarnished arabesques of the wall paper caught his eye. He leaned against the bureau with a sense of loathing. For in the flickering light of the candles the arabesques seemed to writhe and twine-like awakening snakes.

He slammed the window shut. The candles burned steadily. The arabesques were still. He crossed the room, and, conquering his distaste, ran his finger over the surface of the paper. It felt cold and damp. He confessed to no feeling of shame in doing this. As he had told Anderson, he acknowledged nothing, but he was prepared to let commonsense go by the board and to take experiences here at their face value until their causes materialised.

At present this attitude was, in a measure, defensive. At his first entrance in the room he had been aware of a stealthy sense of antagonism. He had felt that he could not find sleep between its tarnished, stained, and damp walls. Now he combated a strong desire to step out of it, to leave the house, to seek whatever there might be of contest in the open. Yet, he remembered, the only open spaces on the island were the clearings here and at the plantation house. Any struggle against the mysteries of Captain's Island must probably take place beneath a roof of ugly memories or in the forest where an unaccountable force unleashed death on its helpless victims.

He turned from the wall. He opened the window again. Although the arabesques resumed their creeping illusion he strangled his revulsion. He placed his revolver beneath the pillow. When he was half undressed he blew out the candles. He climbed into the great bed. He surrendered himself to its soft, dank embrace.

He had only half undressed because he wished to be prepared for any eventuality. He had been sincere in telling Molly that if he was disturbed he would disturb back. Moreover, he anticipated four or five hours of wakefulness until daylight. Four or five hours of waiting. That was what Anderson had said. That was why he was so restless, why his depression had become reasonless, overwhelming. He waited. Yet for what? Anderson, it was clear, had meant apparently supernatural manifestations which came with the night and ceased at dawn.

In an undefined way Miller knew that he waited for more than that-anticipated, in fact, some exceptional adventure that would begin in this house and would end heaven knew where.

He strove uselessly to drive the premonition from his mind. Premonitions, he had always said, were an invention to annoy weak-minded people needlessly. He smiled. Had it come to the point where he was to be so classified? As a matter of fact it should be simple to go to sleep here. Determined to try, he rolled over.

He could not find a comfortable position. Always he combated a tingling desire to hurl the covers back and leap from the chilling depths of this huge bed. And when he closed his eyes the illusion of the arabesques writhed vaguely across the darkness —a circle of snakes, closing in with unsheathed tongues, ready to strike. He wished now that Anderson had never spoken of that fancy.

A sly whispering filled the room-or a hissing? It grew. It died away. It began again. Miller clenched his fists and forced himself to listen calmly, appraisingly. At last he relaxed. That at least was normally explained. The rising wind was setting the cedars in motion. Thus, he told himself, are supernatural stories born and nourished. If he had been so easily moved, what could be expected of ignorant natives like Tony? No doubt it was the type of phenomena to which Anderson and Molly had bared their nerves.

He turned and tried again to sleep, but it was impossible. He had no idea how much time had passed. He had been foolish to blow out the candles. He might have looked at his watch —

All at once he was aware of another noise —a noise he could not mistake. Some one was walking softly, either in the hall, or-it was possible, the footsteps were so nearly inaudible-in his own room, within a few feet of his bed.

He flung back the covers. He sat upright. He listened intently, wishing to be sure, unwilling to make a ridiculous mistake. But there was no doubt. Some one was in his room approaching the bed.

"Who's there?" he muttered.

No answer came. For a moment the sound ceased. Then he heard it again retreating. Outside the whispering of the wind increased. A casement rattled in a sharper gust.

He reasoned. Could these evident footsteps be the pallid tatters of the wall paper flapping in the wind? He remembered they were near the ceiling, while this sound had come from the floor. It appeared now to be in the hall. Then Anderson, Molly, or Tony-Yet none of them would have entered his room in that stealthy fashion, or, entering, would have refused to answer.

Slipping out of bed, he tiptoed to the door. As he had agreed with Molly he had left it open only a crack. Now it stood wide. The wind, he argued, might be responsible. Yet he hurriedly pushed it to. He felt a physical aversion for the black void of the hall where the footsteps strayed.

"Andy!" he said under his breath. "Tony!"

No one answered. The house was completely silent now except for the rattling of the casements.

He returned to the bed, arguing that the footsteps had been imagination or some trickery of the wind, but he could not convince himself.

Little by little, as though the footsteps had started the train, his mind began to play with the thought of a woman's violent death in this room. He knew practically nothing beyond the bare fact. After pampering her, Anderson and the agent had said, Noyer had killed her, had cut her throat; and that had almost certainly happened in this room, perhaps, in this bed, with the arabesques writhing in the candle-light.

He pictured the lawless slaver coming swiftly down that path through the dangerous forest; tramping up the stairs; furiously bursting through that door, which he had just now found mysteriously open; leaning over the bed; killing there that which in his uncouth way he had loved. Had she struggled in the bed? Had she had time to cry out before the great hands had tortured her throat and the knife had flashed?

The theory that the essence of tragedy lingers at the place of its making had never impressed Miller. He did not yield to it now. Yet in spite of his mental struggles, these fancies, these questions persisted. Even the thought of the girl was powerless to guide his imagination to solider ground, although he realised that his future in relation to hers depended on his conquest of a subtle force to which his present experience might, indeed, be traced. He found himself listening for the footsteps again. Were they what Molly awaited when she held her head on one side in an attitude of strained expectancy?

The footsteps did not return, but soon another sound stole into his consciousness —a slow, even, heavy dripping. This time there was no doubt. The sound was in his room, within hand's reach, close to the head of the bed, as though —

He shuddered. He sat upright. The quick motion set the arabesques writhing behind his eyelids. He brushed his hand across his face. He made an effort to regain his sense of proportion. He would find out what that sound was. No matter how much courage it took to reach for his slippers beneath the bed in the vicinity of that sodden, suggestive dripping, he would get up. He would light the candles.

His unwilling fingers found the slippers. He stepped to the floor. He pushed through the inky blackness to the bureau.

The dripping sound followed him. He paused, the match in his hand, wondering if Noyer had heard something like that-had heard and fled from his lifeless, disfigured victim.

Then what he had half expected rang through the echoing house-the cry of a woman, full of terror, strangled, suddenly broken off.

Although he shivered with cold Miller felt the perspiration spring out on his forehead. He struck the match and held it to the candles. The arabesques appeared to twist and twine more violently. The odour from the paper seemed more pungent in spite of the open window. The dripping ceased. He glanced at the floor near the head of the bed, but he saw nothing. It was several minutes before he realised it was Molly who had screamed.

He threw on his clothes, picked up a candle, snatched his revolver from beneath the pillow, and stepped to the hall.

Molly's cry had not been repeated, but something was moving at the foot of the stairs, and he could hear thick breathing. He paused before the door, open a little as Molly had promised. He was afraid to knock, afraid to ask. Finally he forced the words.

"Andy! Molly called —"

Molly's voice, still a little choked, came to him.

"There's something in this room."

Miller pushed the door open.

"Wait!" Anderson commanded in a level, lifeless voice. " There's danger. I said the circle was closing. It is closing."

Miller paused on the threshold. Molly sat up in bed, a dressing gown thrown over her shoulders. Anderson leaned on his elbow.

"Don't come in, Jim," he said. "Listen!"

Miller looked around the room. He spoke reassuringly.

"There's no one-nothing."

"Listen!" Anderson repeated.

Miller heard nothing, so after a moment he stepped into the room. Then he heard —a sound like shot shaken in a crimper.

"They're daring," Anderson said dreamily. "I knew they were growing daring. I was afraid they were getting ready —"

"Andy!" Miller cried. "Pull yourself together!"

He held his revolver in front of him and stooped. He looked under the bed, in the four corners. He could see nothing, but the rattle was repeated.

"You two get out of here," he whispered. "It's safe to step down on this side. But hurry. Get to the hall."

When they had obeyed him he arose, followed them, and closed the door. The rattling came again, apparently from just within the room, yet Miller had seen no snake.

Shaking his head, he led them down the stairs. He found Tony, lying on the steps half way up. The man raised his bearded face to the candle, mouthing horribly.

"I tried to come," he muttered, "I tried —"

"You're not hurt?" Miller asked sharply.

Tony shook his head. He crept backwards down the stairs, his face turned to the light.

The diningroom fire smouldered. As he entered Miller felt a cold breath on his cheek. He hurried through to the kitchen. After a moment he called :

"Tony! Did you open this window?"

He came back.

"Open of those windows-you saw me close it and lock it. You must have opened it, Tony."

Vehemently the native shook his head.

"Did you hear anything come through here?"

"All night," Tony answered, pointing to the hall door," something moving-walking out there."

"And the window in your bedroom," Miller said to Anderson. "That was open, too, but it's high and on the side."

"Jim, remember you didn't see anything," Anderson said softly.

"I'm going through this house from top to bottom," Miller said determinedly. "I shan't sleep again until I know. Make yourselves as comfortable as possible here. Molly, fill that lamp. Let's start this fire up."

He stopped and threw a log on the andirons.

"Did you hear?" Molly asked under her breath.

Still stooping. Miller turned to her. She had assumed again that tense, listening pose.

"What?" he asked.

She put her finger on her lips.

"Outside. Wait. It may come again."

Taut and expectant they waited for several minutes, hearing only the crackling of the fresh log and the moaning of the wind in the chimney. Then Molly raised her hand. A quavering voice reached them, very faintly.

Miller sprang to his feet.

"Stay here," he said.

He ran to the hall, drawing his revolver from his pocket.

"Jim!" Molly cried. " Where are you going?"

"Don't come, Andy," he called," unless I shout."

He flung the front door open and ran into the clearing.

Momentarily the moon swayed free of its enveloping clouds. Abruptly the tiny section of the inlet flashed back its light. There, in a frame of trees with a background of black and ragged dunes, stood the fisherman on the deck of his rotten tub-gigantic, statuesque.

Immediately the clouds snatched the moon back to their obscure embrace. The picture snapped out.

The wind strained and tore past Miller. He could scarcely keep his eyes open to its fury. But he started across the clearing towards the path, for he fancied even in this darkness there was something there at the edge of the clearing. He raised his revolver. He crept forward, muttering to the night :

"Come out! Whoever you are don't try to run back. Come out! Come out!"

A figure threw itself against him and raised warm hands to his face. His arm with the revolver dropped.

"You —" he began.

"I have been at the edge of the forest," the girl said.

"Why are you here?" he asked.

"To tell you to go back. Last night-remember. Tonight you must run this way. The island is not safe."

"Why?" he said. "I shall not run."

"Yes. You must run to the river. You cannot go back this way. You cannot get to the inlet. I didn't think I could get through, but I got through to tell you that. Run to the river. It may be safe there."

"For God's sake," he begged, "tell me what it is."

"The island is full of death tonight."

"Then go to the house. Take the Andersons to the river. There's a boat there."

"Come with me."

"No. I shall stay and fight this death. I have to know what it is. Don't be afraid for me."

He could feel her trembling beneath her heavy black cloak. She dragged at his arm.

"No, no. I love you. I will leave the island with you."

By sheer strength she pulled him a step or two backwards.

"You have lied to me," she said fiercely. "If you loved me you couldn't question now."

Suddenly her face was etched against the darkness. A blue gleam seemed to play over it, to disclose its tortured, passionate terror.

And, as she pulled at his arm, the light reached her wrists. Her wrists were torn and bleeding.

Miller grasped them with a cry and turned. Above the dangerous forest floated a pallid, unnatural light. It was blue. It wavered. It increased. It seemed to fill the sky.

The girl sank to the ground. He tried to raise her, but she drew back.

"It is too late," she said in a dead voice. "You wouldn't listen. There is no hope now."

CHAPTER XVIII
THE PATH TO THE FLAME

Miller slipped his revolver in his pocket and caught the girl up in his arms. As he carried her towards the steps their shadows were flung by the blue light in grotesque distortions across the surface of the coquina house.

He thought she had fainted, but when at the door he stooped and kissed her lips she responded with a quick abandonment.

Anderson waited fretfully in the hall. He threw the door open. Molly was at his back. Tony stood hesitant, just within the diningroom.

"Who —" Anderson began. "The girl! Where —"

"She came with a warning," Miller answered.

Molly cried out:

"What is that light, Jim?"

Anderson ran down the steps.

"The woods have been fired between here and the plantation!"

"No, Andy," Miller called after him. " The light is above the trees. It is not fire."

He carried the girl to a chair in the diningroom.

"Take care of her, Molly. I —"

He broke off. Molly looked at him, guessing the truth. Anderson returned quickly.

"That ghastly light!" he said. "It isn't fire."

Miller pointed at the girl's torn wrists. She quivered before his gesture and tried to hide her hands.

"The wrists again!" Molly whispered.

Tony shrank against the mantel.

"Tell me," Miller demanded, "how were your wrists injured?"

She thrust her wrists behind her back.

"Answer me," he said almost roughly. "Was it coming through that piece of woods?"

She pressed her lips tightly together. There was no colour in her face.

"The one physical clue!" Miller cried "Answer me! Answer me! Do you know how your wrists were torn?"

After a moment she nodded slowly.

"Then tell us! So much depends on that! Tell us!"

She hung her head. She would not answer.

"Tell us!" he begged, "or, after all, are you leagued with the infernal place against us–against me?"

When at last she answered the words came with a dreadful slowness as though their passage tortured her throat.

"No. But I can't tell you that. It would be easier to die than to tell you that."

Her head fell forward. She would not expose her hands, so, although she tried to turn away, the others could see the tears fill her eyes and overflow and drop to her cloak.

Miller stepped aside.

"Molly!" he said softly.

While Molly went to her he drew Anderson to the window. Many shadows thrown by the blue light danced in the clearing.

"There's nothing for it, Andy," he said in an undertone, "I'm going–there,"

"Jim! After all that's happened in those woods?"

"Yes. One is not safe here for that matter. She said so. But the truth is there tonight for the taking,"

He glanced at the girl.

"I have to have the truth. I must clear this up no matter what the risk. But don't worry. If one takes the initiative–you see that's not been done on Captain's Island yet. I shall do it."

"Then, of course," Anderson said, "I shall come with you."

Miller shook his head.

"Molly!" he reminded, "and the girl! I don't have to tell you, Andy-From the first day-You can see for yourself they can't be left. Tony's in a funk-worthless. One of us must go, one must stay. I have more at stake. If I don't come back take them to the boat. Get to Sandport. But I'm not a fool. I'll go carefully-slowly. I've had enough warning. I don't expect to be ambushed by any one-anything."

He threw off Anderson's detaining hand.

"Don't let's have a scene. Don't alarm them. Let me get off quietly. I've a gun for snakes or whatever isn't bullet-proof, and the other thing-what I've heard here-has only hurt my nerves and my pride. It's all right, Andy. That light shines on the key to the whole mystery."

He tiptoed across the floor, but when he reached the hall he heard the girl trying to rise.

"Where is he going! Don't let him go I He must not go! Let me up!"

She screamed:

"Don't let him go!"

Miller threw the screen door open. He sprang into the clearing. He ran swiftly across it.

The wind had risen to a gale. The trees moaned and thrashed in the angry gusts. But the wind, Miller noticed, detached no flames from the blue, light. The whole mass, which was not as large or as high as he had thought at first, swayed bodily in a narrow arc.

When he reached the path that led to the shore where he had left his boat, he was a little sheltered from the wind, and the light, he found, did not penetrate to him.

He went slowly, his hand on the revolver in his pocket. He went silently, recalling that the girl had said the path-to the inlet was closed to him. His care and stealth availed, for he reached the shore without experience.

He paused there for a moment, leaning against the wind which now swept unimpeded across the water. He faced the entrance to the path through the dangerous forest where Jake had died, where Tony last night had been bound by the invisible force. The blue light was strong enough here to show him that entrance —a black cavern, flanked by trees that twisted and strained as though in an agony of warning.

He shrank from stepping between these Dantesque sentinels through that sombre portal.

His mind went to the lantern which he knew lay in the boat only a few feet away. But he had come so far by stealth and silence. Stealthily and silently he must go on. He realised it was his wisest campaign against that which conspired death beyond the frantic trees.

With an effort he stepped forward. Little by little he conquered his revulsion. He entered the path. Again the light failed to reach him. The darkness was like a cloak. It suffocated. In spite of the keen wind tearing past him he could scarcely breathe.

He had no illusions. He knew he was in danger —a danger all the more to be feared because it was uncharted. He slipped his revolver from his pocket. His other hand he carried outstretched before him. Painfully he crept up the path, momentarily expectant of the enemy's first move.

His half serious remark to Anderson about firing this piece of woods came back to him. A match dropped in the dry underbrush at the will of this wind would surrender the forest to a swift destruction. Let the enemy make its first move, let him feel the symptoms of an over-powering lassitude, and he would drop that match, he would yield the woods to that cleansing conflagration.

But the enemy was wary. Its attack did not come. Almost gasping for breath he went on, pushing back the darkness with his outstretched hand as a swimmer cleaves the water.

He knew he must have come half way. He realised he must be in the vicinity of the place where Jake and Tony had been caught, yet he continued unimpeded.

Just beyond, however, he felt a return of the impression that had unnerved him in the co-quina house, that Anderson had described as always lurking there in the dark halls. He knew he was not alone in the forest. There was some presence behind him in the path. He had heard no sound save the tearing of the wind, but he was sure. His retreat had been cut off.

He took his match box from his pocket. If he should sense anything ahead of him, if ho found himself hemmed in, he would fire the woods. There would be light enough then to disclose the nature of the attack.

But while the feeling of a presence in the rear persisted, he received no warning from the front. He knew the ruins must be near. In the semicircle of the slave quarters he would feel safer. He would be able to see the light from there, to study it, perhaps, to detect its source. Only a few steps morel

He stumbled. The underbrush snatched at his legs. He was off the path. He stopped abruptly, his throat contracting, on the point of striking his match. But a saving thought came to him. He turned to the right. The blue light played faintly there. He understood. He had reached the end of the path. Instead of turning with it through the ruins he had plunged straight ahead into the thicket.

Carefully picking his way, he regained the path and ran between the ruins into the semicircle. He had passed unmolested through the dangerous forest. He looked around. The light flickered now above the double row of trees that lined the avenue. It had grown very faint. While he looked at it, puzzled, at a loss, it faded out. The wind seemed to gather greater strength as though the passing of the light had unleashed its last restraint.

Miller was bewildered. Had his initiative, indeed, made itself felt and driven the solution beyond his reach? A reaction swept him. At the moment when he had fancied his hand at the throat of the mystery he was suddenly left as helpless as ever. In a burst of irritation he questioned if he, as well as the Andersons, was not the victim of some gigantic hoax. He brushed the question aside. There had been no trickery about the girl's emotion or her fear for him.

He thought of going on to the plantation house, of arousing Morgan, of telling him of the injury to the girl's wrists, of her terror, and of her warning; yet that might involve her in difficulties he could not foresee. Should he then retrace his steps through the forest and return empty-handed to the coquina house?

In the first place he did not want to go back through the forest before daylight. He had keyed himself to the strain of traversing it when he had expected to achieve a solution of the mystery. Now the strain was broken. And he recalled the sense of a presence behind him in the path.

He was aware of that sense again, so strongly that he glanced over his shoulder. He could see nothing. The darkness was absolute.

The idea came to him that some clue might hide within these ugly ruins. He had never had an opportunity to explore them, yet they must have sheltered the worst horrors of Noyer's reign, and they bounded that piece of forest. He stepped forward. This definite objective tautened his courage. He walked faster. He had almost reached the door of the nearest of the quarters when the light flashed again. Only this time it was white and overwhelming. He felt himself consumed in its vicious flames. Immediately it snapped out. His consciousness went out with it.

CHAPTER XIX
WITHIN THE CIRCLE

He lay apparently for a long time while his memory stirred and his mind reluctantly resumed its functions.

He recalled the beginning of the night at the coquina house, the sounds and feelings that had disturbed him there, the cry from outside, the picture of the silent fisherman, erect against the dunes, the warning of the girl, the blue light, her terror, his journey through the woods, his determination to seek a clue in the ruins.

Where was he now? He lay in utter darkness. The rushing of the wind was as fierce as ever.

Then, gently at first, he heard a sound from the black cloak of the night-the sound he had heard in Anderson's bedroom, the sound that had shared so often in the island's manifestations. It was not far away-only six or seven feet, he thought-and straight ahead. After a moment the rattle came again. This time it was answered from the rear. It was taken up on either side. It rose. It died away. Its volume grew again. An acrid, loathsome odour reached his nostrils. He lay within a circle of snakes; and, although from the lack of pressure he knew he was not bound, he was powerless to move.

He choked back the cry that tore at his throat. His mind was clearer now. He forced it to work logically. If he was not bound why was it impossible for him to move? He recalled the white light. An explanation of his helplessness ran hotly to his brain. Meantime the revolting prophecy of the rattling continued. While he fancied the deadly circle was closing, he set his will to work. He succeeded in twitching the fingers of one hand. Actually it was not much more than a minute after his return to consciousness when he drew his knees up and raised himself to a sitting posture.

He patted the ground at his side. It was hard like packed earth. Certainly he was not in the forest. Then —?"

Fighting the racking pains that ran through his head and body, he reached in his pocket for his revolver and his match box. The revolver was gone. He had been carrying it when the white light had flashed. Of course it had fallen from his hand. The match box, however, was there. He took out a match and scraped it. In answer to the slight noise the rattling rose excitedly.

The match blinded him at first, but before it was half burned out his eyes accustomed themselves to its light. He glanced quickly around. He saw no snakes.

He was in the centre of a small, bare room whose floor, as he had thought, was of packed earth. The flame played on rough grey walls. It failed to disclose the top of a peaked roof. He noticed a line of brushwood, perhaps two feet high, which ran around all four walls. Unquestionably the snakes lurked behind that screen. Why did they not come out to converge on him? When would they come out?

Just before the match expired he saw a closed oak door in the wall to his left.

He knew now that he was in one of the slave quarters which he had started to explore-probably in one of those which yesterday he had noticed had been repaired. But how had he come there? And why was he left surrounded by snakes which did not attack? Now that he felt himself placed at the heart of the mystery he could not stop to reason. His danger was too apparent. He must reach the oak door. He must escape from the circle.

With painful effort he raised himself to his knees. He was by no means sure he could stand upright, yet he must try. He must get to the door.

He paused on his knees. Something moved at the door. It must have been opened a little, for a streak of yellow light cut across the left hand wall. He waited, breathing heavily. It was as though his return to consciousness and his determination to escape had been known, and that this sickly light was a warning that the door was watched, that escape was impossible.

The streak grew. It reached the further wall. The door was thrown wide. Framed on the threshold; Miller saw the great figure of the fisherman.

For a moment he stood there, staring at Miller in the light of the lantern he held. His eyes had the same fixed look Miller had remarked before. His lips were pressed tightly together.

So Anderson's instinct had been right! The fisherman was at the bottom of it. Probably he had done for Jake. But Tony! Tony had seen no one.

Miller was unwilling to believe. The absence of motive, the wanton cruelty, these elaborate preparations! A mad thought came to him. Could there be any connection between this figure and the giant slaver, long since dead? He spoke with difficulty.

"What—does all this mean? Will you help me out of here?"

The fisherman's stare did not waver.

"These snakes!" Miller whispered.

The fisherman's face showed no change. It was such a face as one might fancy beneath the mask of an executioner.

Miller struggled to his feet. He swayed. He attempted to step forward.

Now the fisherman moved. He whipped a cord from his pocket and threw his great bulk towards Miller.

Miller raised his fists. He tried to hold the figure off, but his strength was nothing against this giant. He went to the floor. A knee was on his chest. Like a child he was rolled from side to side while the cord was fastened around his arms and legs.

"What are you going to do?" Miller gasped.

The fisherman arose and walked to the wall. He kicked a portion of the brushwood away, disclosing a square pine box. He turned to the corner. He lifted a long, slender pole which stood there. Miller saw that a cord ran down the pole and made a loop at the lower end.

The fisherman returned to the box, and, using the end of the pole, raised the lid. An angry rattling came from the box. The fisherman thrust the pole inside.

"What are you going to do?" Miller repeated.

The fisherman did not turn. Carefully, systematically he moved the end of the pole with the loop backwards and forwards in the box. One hand clutched the cord near the top of the pole, after a moment drew it tight, then slowly raised the pole until the end with the loop was above the edge of the box.

The flat head of a snake was caught in the loop. Its bead-like eyes gleamed in the lantern light. They found Miller's eyes and rested there. The forked tongue darted in and out of the revolting and venomous mouth.

Miller strained at his bonds. He could not move his hands or his feet the fraction of an inch.

"Let me up. What are you going to do?" he asked with dry lips.

The fisherman continued to raise the pole until the snake's circular, shining body curled and flapped about his legs. Miller watched, fascinated. While the body thrashed, the head, caught in the loop, remained still. The evil eyes did not leave his.

The fisherman turned and stepped towards Miller. He lowered the pole until the snake's body was beating the floor with soft, abhorrent strokes until the head almost rested on the packed earth.

With a deliberate slowness the fisherman brought the snake closer to Miller. It tried to get its head free to coil. When this sly, snail-like march was arrested close to Miller's bound and helpless body the fisherman would slip the loop and spring back. Then the snake would coil. In its anger it would strike at what was nearest.

Inch by inch this slow death, whose every step he could foresee, approached. The tiny eyes held him. It seemed impossible that the reasonless fury behind them could project to him the supreme unconsciousness. He shuddered.

"Man! You can't do this!"

He wet his lips.

"Or—then Faster! Faster!"

For the first time the mask-like face of the fisherman altered. The tight lips parted. They stretched in a distorted smile. He took another step forward. The snake was very near.

The evil of the smile aroused Miller. He forced his eyes from the snake's. The girl, whom he would never see again if this torturing execution was carried out, flashed through his mind. He saw her as she had been that first morning on the beach, in her white robe, bent to the wind, gazing out to sea. He remembered her just now in the coquina house, hiding her bleeding wrists, crying out that they must not let him go. She had known then that he would risk death. Did she know it would come to him here and in this fashion? Hope was born. He could not analyse her attitude, her refusal to tell what she knew of these horrors of the island, of her own connection with them; but she could not, after that warning, after that abandonment on the steps, let him end like this. She must have conquered whatever forces had held her from speaking. She must have indicated to Anderson, Tony, and Molly what he faced. If she had done that, those friends, he knew, would not take the road to the river and the boat And the fisherman probably did not guess that she had been to the coquina house. So he smiled back, and he cried out at the top of his lungs :

"Andy! Tony!"

If they came even after the snake had struck there might be time for a tourniquet, for some antidote. At least he would have a chance.

The travesty of a smile left the fisherman's face. He paused. He glanced towards the half open door. Miller looked, too, expectantly, and he saw Morgan run in. There was no humour in the genial little man's face now. He stopped dead, and drew back. His lips twitched nervously.

"Morgan!" Miller cried.

Morgan spoke with a distinct effort There was a note of helplessness in his voice.

"You, Miller, trapped! My heavens! How did this happen?"

"Don't ask questions," Miller said. "Thank the Lord you're here. Get me up. Get me away from that snake."

Morgan stared at him. The fisherman kept his eyes on the little man. At last Morgan pressed his hands together then spread them in a wide gesture.

"I can do nothing, Miller. This is pretty tough."

"What do you mean?" Miller cried.

Morgan hung his head.

"Just that. I'm helpless to save you. If you'd only come to spend the night with me as I asked! You'd be safe in bed now."

"You mean —" Miller gasped. "It's impossible!"

"I can't tell you what I mean," Morgan answered.

"Tell me," Miller begged.

Morgan turned away.

"No-not even to dead men."

The fisherman still watched. At last Morgan made a quick gesture. The fisherman's fingers twitched at the cord which imprisoned the snake's head. Then his hand grew rigid.

"Better not!"

Morgan and the fisherman swung around at the quiet command which Miller had hoped for, had almost felt sure would come.

"Andy," he said with a trembling laugh, "Don't shout 'hands up' until you've put a charge of shot in that snake."

Anderson stepped inside.

"Cover them, Tony," he said.

Tony entered, raising his revolver. Anderson lowered his shot-gun and fired.

Miller saw a piece of flaming wadding from the shell bury itself in the brushwood, but his relief at watching the snake's body torn by the shot drove everything else for the moment from his mind.

The fisherman tossed the pole and the shattered snake behind him. He turned as though for guidance to Morgan; but Morgan, his face twisted again, faced the revolver with which Tony threatened him.

"Don't lose sight of that fisherman, Andy," Miller said. "Keep an eye on him while you cut this rope."

Anderson stooped and cut the cord. He helped Miller to his feet.

"Morgan?" Anderson said. "What does this mean?"

"He's been asking that." Morgan answered. "Well, find out if you can. I can't tell you."

"I've found out one thing-how Jake died. It's murder, Morgan."

"You try to connect me with that!"

"I'll try. And this attempt —"

"Fortunately he wasn't hurt," Morgan answered.

"My story," Miller said, "and the evidence of these snakes, collected here, will hurt!"

"Evidence! There goes that evidence."

He pointed to the brushwood in the corner where the flaming wadding from Anderson's gun had fallen. The brushwood was beginning to blaze. Miller tried to stamp it out, but the twigs were like tinder. They crackled in the fire that quickly swept the length of the wall. The rattling of the snakes, just now menacing, arose in a staccato appeal. In a moment the fire would be at the door.

"Take these two out and keep them covered," Miller said. "Don't let them get away. We'll reach the bottom of this business now,"

He followed the others into the gale-swept semicircle. The fire was through the doorway almost at his heels. It licked its way in the dry grass along the wall towards the opening between the quarters. There the wind would catch it finally and deliver to its hungry tongues the evil piece of woods.

As the flames rose the trees of the avenue sprang into gargantuan, twisted motion. Through their straining branches the rear of the plantation house gleamed white. The flames also showed Miller the backs of Molly and the girl, seated on a fallen log at the side of the avenue. The girl's head was hidden on Molly's shoulder. He looked away. The difficulty of the situation stifled him. Her father involved in this brutal scandal! Undoubtedly she had saved his life, yet what was her own share?

He swung on Morgan angrily.

"Answer my questions. Explain this business."

"I can explain nothing," Morgan answered. "As far as I am concerned there's nothing to explain beyond the fact that I found you in the hands of that giant and told you the obvious thing that I couldn't handle him and get you away. What do I know 1 These natives I Their purposes are beyond me. You people seem determined to incriminate me somehow or other. That's nonsense. Let's be sensible and go to the house and have a drink while Rome burns."

Miller grasped Morgan's arm. He shook it savagely.

"You say I'm too determined. Understand, I'm determined to find out what it is you won't tell even to dead men-why you've played this Judas part, why you've put the Andersons on the rack, why you killed Jake, why you tried to kill Tony and me. And I'll find out. There isn't a rat-hole in that house of yours I won't search for a reason. And your daughter! Look at her sitting there."

Morgan turned wildly.

"My daughter!"

"She warned me," Miller said. "She saved my life. Even if your fisherman is a sphinx, do you think she'll keep silent now?"

Morgan's jaw dropped. An animal-like cry left his mouth. As Tony, momentarily surprised, lowered his revolver, Morgan ran to the corner of the building, sprang across the flames now blazing there, and leaped into the tangled undergrowth.

Tony raised his arm. He aimed at the broad back. Miller struck the gun up.

"No, Tony. It isn't necessary."

For as Morgan had jumped, the wind had seized the flames and had leaped shrieking with them into the forest after his retreating figure. The thicket crackled like a scattered skirmish line. The fire licked along the trunks to the waving tree tops. The glare became blinding.

Miller turned gravely to Anderson.

"That thicket will hold him back like a thousand hands. Perhaps it's better than he deserved. You and Tony take that tongue-tied fellow to the plantation house. I'll bring Molly and th- the girl."

He walked slowly, reluctantly to the fallen log where the two sat with their backs still turned. He touched the girl's bowed head. He spoke gently :

"Your-your father got away."

Her head went a little lower. He had to stoop to catch her answer.

"He is not my father."

She said no more. He did not have the heart to question her then.

They entered the plantation house through the kitchen. They saw no one. A lamp turned low burned in the library-that same dim eye that had regarded Miller the night he had sailed into the inlet. They left Molly and the girl there and debated in the hall what disposition to make of their prisoner. Miller suggested the cupola.

"Noyer rigged it up," he said, "as a corrective for his house servants. We can't lock him in, but it has wrist and leg irons. I dare say we would be justified."

It was the best expedient. With the revolver at his back the silent fisherman climbed willingly enough.

Miller set his lantern on the floor of the cupola. He raised one of the irons by its chain. He started. He stooped swiftly. He held the iron close to the light and examined it.

"Andy," he cried. "Look here!"

The edge of the iron was wet. Miller ran his finger around it. When he held his finger up it was stained red.

"They had her here," he said," chained in this place! She must have known what was on foot and refused to share in it. Their only excuse for such barbarity would be to keep her from coming to us. Her wrists are small. You can see. She managed to pull them through and escape. My heavens, Andy 1 The humiliation! If he wasn't her father he had a father's place. No wonder she wouldn't tell us how her wrists were hurt."

He raised his eyes to the fisherman.

"You silent devil! I'll find a way to make you speak when I get you in a courtroom."

Anderson picked up another set of irons.

"We're justified. Anything is justified," he said, "only I wish it was Morgan we had."

The fisherman made no effort at resistance. He stood stoically while they placed the irons around his wrists and ankles, and screwed the bolts tight.

"They fit him well enough," Miller said. "No chance of his slipping out of them."

He brought his face close to the fisherman's. He stared into the unwinking eyes.

"Do you realise you're likely to swing for this business?"

But the mask-like face did not alter. The huge shoulders did not tremble.

"It's no use," Miller said; "he won't talk."

Anderson started down the ladder, but Miller's eyes were attracted to the floor. After a moment he called Anderson back.

"What do you suppose this powder is, Andy?"

He pointed to a few yellow grains directly beneath the trap in the roof of the cupola. The chain which held the fisherman to the wall clanked. Miller looked up. The man's face had at last altered. Its quality of a mask had been destroyed by a positive emotion, and that emotion was fear.

"It means something," Miller cried triumphantly. "By Jove! I believe I can guess what."

While Anderson and Tony pressed close, and the fisherman, his face blank again, looked on, Miller bent down and scraped the grains into a little heap.

"Looks like sand," Anderson said.

"I've seen such sand before," Miller answered," on the Fourth of July for instance."

He took his match box, struck a match, and touched it to the powder. The yellow grains hissed. They sprang into a brilliant blue flame. The flame died, leaving a tiny mass of carbon on the floor.

"The blue light!" Anderson cried.

"Andy, Tony, lift me up here."

They raised him to the trap in the roof. He pushed it back and put his head and shoulders through. After a moment he lowered a long, rusty iron rod to whose end was fastened an old-fashioned brazier protected by wire netting.

"Look at this relic," Miller said when he was on the floor again; "something from Noyer's days."

He held the brazier so he could glance in its top.

"From the amount of carbon here it was kept well filled tonight. It was a signal, Andy. For what? For those wild oystermen —"

He nodded at the fisherman.

"Probably friends and accomplices of his."

He grew thoughtful.

"The girl knows, but I hate to put her on the stand now."

"I think she knows everything," Anderson replied.

"I'm not so sure of that," Miller said. "But she knows why this light was burned. Anyhow we've done all we can here. Go on down. We haven't been through the servants' rooms yet. There's Morgan's man and his cook. If they're still here we may get something out of them."

They found, however, only the woman. Evidently terrified by the fire, she had buried her head beneath the covers and lay there, shivering and-when they shook her and questioned her-almost incoherent.

Miller, disappointed, stared from the window. The entire sky in the southwest appeared to be in flames. But he fancied the fire would burn itself out in the marshes, that the coquina house would be spared. He hoped for that. In the light of what they already knew they might find something there of value. He was almost afraid now that the fire would destroy too much. He turned back to the woman impatiently.

"At least you ought to be able to tell us where the man is-Morgan's man."

"I don't know," she answered.

"He has the next room. Didn't you hear him go out?"

"Yes-about eleven o'clock, but I don't know where."

"Look here," Miller said; "is he anything to you? Are you —"

"He's my husband," she answered.

"And he didn't tell you where he was going?"

"No. I'm afraid. I'm —Why do you ask me? I'm the one that wants to know."

"Nothing to be had here," Miller said. "We'd better scatter. I told Morgan I'd search every rat-hole in the place and he let me see plainly enough he didn't like the idea. It's worth a chance. We may turn up something. We'll meet in the library."

When Miller entered the library empty-handed an hour later, he found Anderson and Tony already there. They, too, had been unsuccessful.

"We thought we'd wait until you came before beginning on this room," Anderson said.

Miller glanced around. The girl lay on the sofa, her face to the wall. She had not looked up at his entrance. Molly sat near her in an easy chair.

"Is she asleep?" Miller asked Molly in a whisper.

Molly shook her head.

Miller approached the sofa. He hesitated before the apparently lifeless figure. After a moment he turned to the others.

"Let's see what's in this room first," he said, "then —"

He broke off, staring at the high bookshelves, piled with musty black-bound volumes.

"These old books!" he cried. " These dry, valueless reports, as Morgan called them! This room was where Morgan spent most of his time. We can only try,"

He walked to the shelves and commenced pulling down the boobs, handing them to Tony and Anderson who placed them on the floor. There was nothing behind them but smooth, unpapered walls and an accumulation of dust.

Facing failure here, too, he hurried his task. He picked up several volumes at once and carelessly passed them to the others. His carelessness grew with his disappointment. A book fell to the floor from a pile he was handing to Anderson. He heard something click on the boards. He glanced down. The light of the lamp was caught there and flashed up into his eyes.

Miller stooped quickly. Anderson and Tony were already on their knees before the open book. Molly leaned forward with an exclamation.

The book was very thick. A hole had been scooped in its pages in such a manner that it would leave no trace when the book was closed. Curled in this nest lay a string of perfectly matched diamonds.

Anderson picked it up. As it uncurled, its myriad facets caught the light and sparkled. It seemed almost conscious of this superb exposition of its value.

"It's worth thousands," Anderson gasped. "I wouldn't dare say how much."

But Miller was not gazing with the others at the necklace. His eyes were drawn by the girl who had started uneasily and had buried her head deeper in her arms. He turned slowly back to the others.

"It's worth your peace of mind," he said. "It's the whole answer."

CHAPTER XXI

THE MENACE OF THE SLAVE QUARTERS

Molly came forward and knelt with them over the volumes from which an academic odour of stale leather arose.

"Yes," Miller said, "we must run through every one of these books."

For long periods they worked without reward, but occasionally a book would disclose a cunningly scooped nest sheltering some costly setting of rich stones. When the last one had been examined they arranged their discoveries on the table. Morgan, doubtless, had often set them so to gloat over them late at night when he had fancied himself secure, while the Andersons, perhaps, were battling against the manifestations of the coquina house.

There were thirty pieces in all of various worth.

"I don't know much about such things," Anderson said. " Molly, what do you think!"

"Two hundred thousand at the very least," she answered, a little awed by the display.

Miller leaned against the mantel, staring at the glittering row.

"You can figure the duty on this stuff," he said, "and probably it's only one side of the scheme. Andy, Andy, we ought to have seen it all from the beginning."

Molly looked at him inquiringly.

"I don't know how. Morgan was the last man to suspect of anything like this."

"Yes, but Andy himself told me enough the night I got here to have put the whole thing in our hands if we had only reasoned. I don't know what there is about a suspicion of the supernatural that knocks one's reason into a cocked hat. You go against it with a certain mathematical contempt as I started down here. That's it. You face the supernatural with a chip on your shoulder. Your fight is likely to be negative. Your first concern is to prove that a fact is not supernatural rather than to find out why it seems supernatural. It's the doubt of the unexplored that subconsciously affects the soundest of us. We've been told so often of the existence of forces that play across the barrier of death that we are afraid, almost unknown to our reasoning selves, of the possibility of conviction. For that matter the climate of this place, and its lonely, depressing atmosphere are enough to foster superstition. That required no trickery. That was all in his favour. And your talk of what you had suffered here, Tony's overwhelming belief and fear, and Morgan's carefully planned allusions-creeping allusions from the sanest, the most material of types! —All that was enough to make one doubt, even though he told himself, as I did, that there was no doubt."

"We tried, Jim," Anderson answered. " We turned every stone. His scheme was too carefully planned, too subtle for us."

"Yes, and as Molly says, it was not easy to suspect Morgan. He was too convincing a fellow victim. Then when we did turn from the unknown it was only to the unseen, to those oystermen that we knew were not far off in the marshes, and the possibility of some connection between the fisherman and them."

"But how, Jim," Molly asked, "could you have foreseen anything like this?"

"Andy told me the history of Noyer and his island," he answered. "Since the days of the buccaneers, when they dared bring their ships in here to careen them, it has offered a refuge for lawlessness. He also spoke of that fisherman's tub, moving silently through the water at night. That meant a new, expensive engine in a worthless boat; and no one was allowed on that boat. Noyer could smuggle slaves in here unmolested after the law had made it a deadly crime, because, as Andy explained, the island was completely isolated. He was king of it and of this inlet and of this lonely coast. Is the island any less isolated now than it was then? Isn't the dweller in this plantation house as much of a king now as Noyer was before the war-provided, of course, that the coquina house doesn't shelter strangers? Morgan had heard the history of the place, and, since he was out for that sort of thing, it suggested the ideal opportunity-everything. There is only a third rate revenue officer in Martinsburg, and this coast has seen no smuggling since before the war. The island has been uninhabited since then. Now a respectable northern family makes la winter home of it. There wasn't the slightest ground for suspicion. It was ideal except for you and Molly. Your renting of the coquina house was the fly in the ointment. And you must confess it was hard on Morgan when both places had stood empty for fifty years. You can imagine his fury. He had to get you out of that house and off the island."

"Yes," Anderson agreed, "from his point of view we had to go. He had to have a clear field. But, Jim, you heard yourself there in the coquina house!"

"Yes, but inevitably that was the lever he'd use-the supernatural for which the island was notorious, with its rotten loneliness to back it, and the decayed, unhealthy atmosphere of the coquina house. You see he had time after he heard you were coining to arrange the trickery of your house to his fancy. He did it cleverly. Since you discovered nothing, we'll have to grant him that."

He glanced at the girl.

"Perhaps we can be guided to the tools. But I think probably in that thicket back of the kitchen —"

He stepped to the table and fingered the jewellery.

"He had to take chances. He was ready to go any length. There's more profit in this stuff, you know, than there ever was in flesh and blood. And I wouldn't be surprised if there was larger merchandise-furs, for instance. He was the man to do it on a huge scale, to squeeze the last drop from his opportunity."

"Then where —" Anderson began.

"Certainly not in the house. It has no cellar, and he had to keep it free for your friendly visits. I'm afraid we'll never see that evidence. It was probably stored in the slave quarters, in the ones he had repaired. The fire —"

He broke off, looking at Tony. Understanding flashed from the native's eyes. He wanted to speak.

"What is it, Tony?"

The native's lips parted. He pointed towards the ruined slave quarters.

"It was kept there," he said.

"How can you be sure of that?" Miller asked.

"I saw it. I didn't know then."

"Tony! You idiot! And you never spoke! When?"

"Th-the night I was caught in the woods. I don't know how that happened, but —"

Miller glanced significantly at Anderson.

"He was caught, as he calls it, after he had seen enough to give the whole game away. But why didn't he know? Why did he see no one? Tony, why didn't you tell me you had discovered the loot?"

"I only saw big packing cases. I guessed it was furniture they hadn't unpacked. I didn't think any more about it 'til now."

"Tell us how it happened. Talk now. Make yourself talk."

The native swayed from foot to foot, embarrassed, unaccustomed and unhappy in the centre of the stage.

"I was waiting for you at the end of the avenue. It was light then. I wasn't afraid. I reckoned I'd stand outside and peek through the window-they tell such stories about the quarters, you know. And it was daylight. I sorter dared myself. I went over. The window was broken. An old rag hung over it. I pushed it away. There were these packing cases. There was writing on them. I was going to read that, but somebody was coming out of the kitchen and down the avenue."

He stopped and wet his lips.

"Go on," Miller urged.

"That's all. That's all I saw."

"All you saw! But how did you get there in the woods, practically unconscious, unable to move!"

"I told you," he answered. "A little after that it got dark and I was frightened. I started down the path to the boat. I don't know."

"But what happened before that-after you had looked in the window? Who was it disturbed you by coming out of the kitchen?"

"The woman-the cook."

"Did she speak to you?"

"Yes."

"Well-what!"

"She told me Mr. Morgan had said I was to have a jolt of whiskey."

Miller grasped Anderson's arm.

"That's it! Of course he had been watched. And you drank it! Did you drink it all?"

"Oh, I ain't thought much of that. Maybe half. I'm not much of a whiskey drinker."

"Half of it, you see! It worked slowly. He wasn't drugged blind. Probably he lost himself for only a few minutes. They caught him in the woods and bound him in case he should come out of it before the snake had finished him. He began to come out. That wouldn't have made any difference, but they heard the girl and me talking by the ruins. They didn't know how much she was telling me. It was probably Morgan's man and the fisherman. They may have been unarmed. Perhaps they thought I might charge down the path prepared for them. They didn't dare risk it. It was easier to throw Morgan down and let their share in the smuggling come out than to face a murder charge. So they flung his cords off. It was the looped snake he heard rattling. That's why Morgan rushed out to the boat the next morning-to find out what I knew. He saw he was safe."

He smiled mirthlessly.

"By and by, Tony, you'll be ashamed to look a ghost in the face. You ought to be ready now to go to Sandport. Are you?"

The man nodded sheepishly.

"That's right," Anderson said. "This was evidently to be a big haul. The authorities ought to be warned. They might catch the man and possibly those alleged brothers in the river or the marshes."

"Take Morgan's' launch," Miller directed, "and swing around to the beach where we left the dingy. The fire's gone to the right. You ought to find the path open to the river end of the island. Take the boat you hired this afternoon and rouse Sandport. Tell them to send a fast launch to Martinsburg with the news, and to do what they can themselves."

When Tony had gone, still shame-faced but reluctant in spite of it, Miller walked over to the girl. He touched her shoulder hesitatingly.

"I am sorry," he said. "But you see what we know already."

She turned. Her eyes were red from weeping. Her lips drooped.

"You were there that night," he said softly. "You warned me not to go through the path, therefore you knew what they were doing with Tony."

She did not answer. He spread his arms helplessly.

"I don't want to believe these things."

She spoke. Her voice was scarcely more than a whisper.

"I wasn't waiting-to warn you at first."

He sat on the edge of the sofa.

"Then you didn't know it was to be done."

"No. I knew other things, but I didn't know that. While I waited I saw him stumble down the path. I saw them follow swiftly with the snake in a loop. It came to me all at once how the other man had died,"

"You must have known those snakes were kept there."

"They told me the fisherman caught them to sell their skins in Martinsburg. They are valuable. I believed that. I wanted to save the man, but you were the only one to whom I could turn, and that meant probably killing him-my uncle. But when you came I only thought of saving you. I knew if you went down that path and discovered them they would try to kill you, too."

"Yes," Miller said, "they would have done that if they could. It would have been necessary."

"But murder!" Anderson said. "These cunning preparations for death, always ready, always waiting!"

"Essential from Morgan's point of view," Miller said. "He regretted it, but it was that or get out and let the whole scheme go to blazes. Until he drove you off the island he had to be prepared. He couldn't keep your household from his under the circumstances of your loneliness and propinquity without arousing suspicion at the start. Therefore, if any of you stumbled on the evidence that would ruin him and send the lot of them to jail, your silence had to be assured. He had used one of the island's curses, its superstition, to help the climate drive you out. For death, if it was necessary, he chose the other, its poisonous snakes. If any one was found dead of snake-bite in such a place, why should he or any man be suspected? He didn't miss the value of a single card, but I'll do him the credit of saying he hoped he wouldn't have to play that one. But you wouldn't be driven out. Then the other day Jake saw too much, and his friends, the cook and the man, clinked glasses with him."

"Horrible!" Molly said; "and if she hadn't told us, guided us, you, too, Jim —"

"Yes," he answered softly. "I know."

He turned back to the girl.

"But when you came to the beach the next morning you evaded my questions. You told me things that were not quite true."

She sat up. The colour came back to her face.

"Yon can't misunderstand that now-The struggle, the dreadful uncertainty of the road I ought to follow! I hoped to persuade you to leave the island, for I knew you would try to find out, and sooner or later they would kill you, I tried to make myself tell you everything, but I couldn't, I couldn't. He was my uncle-the only father I have ever known. I was given to him a baby, when my mother died. And I loved him. We were happy until this trouble in New York."

She stopped and looked down.

"He hinted at some money trouble," Miller urged gently.

"Yes. He had a good jewellery business. Then the government fined him heavily for evading customs duties. He paid the fine, but it drove him into bankruptcy. He swore he would get even with the government. It became a passion."

"Then you knew his plan when you came here!"

"No, oh, no. Don't think I'm bad."

Molly seated herself beside her on the sofa and took her hand. The girl glanced at her gratefully, wonderingly.

"I knew nothing at first. He made excuses for introducing those two men as his brothers to the Andersons. One had been his partner. The other was in the same business. He told me things that weren't true about the Andersons. That was why I wouldn't be friendly even at first, why I held them away. Sooner or later I had to discover everything. That day came. I suffered alone. I tried to find the right thing to do. You don't know the unhappiness of that time. What was I to dot There was no one to whom I could go. And I had no money. I couldn't leave the island, and I couldn't betray him. One doesn't find it easy to betray a father. It was the same thing. So I went to him and begged him to give it up. I couldn't move him. In the end he made me promise."

"I see," Miller said. "That was why you told me he had stayed because of you."

"Yes, because I had promised not to betray him. Do you blame me for that?"

"I blame you for nothing," he said softly, "unless it is that you tried to hold me away from you too."

"I had to, yet I failed. I wanted no friends here, and you see I was right. You see how it has worked out."

"Why were you treated so brutally tonight!" Molly asked.

"Because I knew the boat was coming tonight. It was to be the biggest stroke. I tried to make him promise there would be no murder. He wouldn't promise. He said he would send the man to the coquina house at midnight. He said he would try to keep you interested there, so you wouldn't hear anything outside and be tempted to meddle. But he swore if you did meddle you would have to pay his price. Then I told him I couldn't let it go on. I couldn't risk it. I took back my promise. I said I would warn you. I started to run out of the house."

She raised her torn wrists to her face.

"He lost his temper. It was terrible."

After a moment she continued.

"But I got free. Without their knowing it I went to the edge of the clearing at the coquina house. I made up my mind to stay there all night, and, if you heard anything, if you ran out, to keep you from coming this way where the danger was. Then some one called from the boat and you came. When the blue light burned I knew it was too late. I knew you would take your life in your hands to find out what the blue light was."

"We know it was a signal," Anderson began, "but —"

Miller raised his hand.

"Understand," he said to the girl, "I appreciate —I know the strain. I hate to put you on the rack, but the fisherman —I've tried. He won't talk."

"No," she said. "He wouldn't anyway. But he is dumb."

"Dumb!"

"Yes. That was why they used him. Because of that he has been an outcast. He hates normal men. The rest were my uncle's own people. He could trust them. Well-my uncle is dead. Oh, I know! If you wish, I think I have a way of making the fisherman speak, and, since there is much that I can't tell you —"

"How?" Miller asked.

"It isn't —I don't like —I've succeeded with him easily before. When we first came my uncle asked me to do it. I thought it was fun then, but later I understood why it was."

She hesitated. She sighed.

"It makes no difference," she said. "I'll do what you wish. Where is he?"

"In the cupola. Will you come?"

She arose, stood unsteadily for a moment, then walked across the room. Miller took the lamp. He helped her up the stairs. Anderson and Molly followed.

Miller placed the lamp on the floor. The fisherman's eyes blinked at first, but as they grew accustomed to the light his countenance resumed its statuesque expression.

The girl faced him. She looked in his eyes. She spoke to him quietly, soothingly. Her voice went on with a droning quality. Suddenly Miller understood. He understood, too, the barrier she had tried to raise between them when he had startled her that first morning on the beach. He could define now the sense of unreasoning contest that had swept him when she had suggested his inability to hold her, to find her lips. It was her trick, natural or acquired, that she had used to save herself the torture of seeming friendship with the Andersons, that she had flung with all her will to avoid an acquaintanceship and its possible complications with him, the newcomer. But his own will had been too strong. It had always accepted the challenge.

"Where did you learn that?" he whispered.

She motioned him to be quiet. After a few moments she began to question. The right arm of the fisherman slowly rose at her command while the fingers flashed the short-hand of the dumb.

In a dreamy voice, as though she were almost hypnotic herself, she translated these signals. They told how the goods had been shipped by Morgan's accomplice in Europe to one of the Bahama Islands; how the brothers had gone there in their small schooner with a Jamaican crew, received the goods, stowed them away in a miscellaneous cargo, and cleared for Martinsburg; how it had always been arranged for the schooner to reach the inlet bar in the middle of the night, when the fisherman would slip out in his silent tug and take off the boxes; how the blue signal light was burned as a necessity to give the schooner her course for the mouth of the river and to guide the fisherman to the entrance of the risky channel across the inlet bar.

Tonight, she translated, the storm had alarmed the fisherman. He had not dared wait for the light. He had taken his chances and come on in. One of the brothers had come with him. He supposed he had taken alarm and had escaped with the boat. As for himself, the blue light had shown him Miller on the shore, hesitating before the entrance to the dangerous forest. He had followed him, and, when Miller was about to enter the forbidden quarters, had struck him on the temple from behind. Locking him in the building with the snakes, he had delayed for a time the necessary execution while he had tried unsuccessfully to find Morgan.

She turned to them wearily.

"There is nothing else, is there?"

Miller shook his head. He walked to the rear window of the cupola. The flames had done their work quickly. Only a red glow hung sombrely over a blackened desert. It failed to reach the clouds where the skirmishers of the dawn with quiet confidence fought it back.

"There's nothing else," he said. "Bring him out of it."

He went down the ladder, beckoning to Molly and Anderson. When they were in the lower hall he took their hands.

"Would you mind?" he asked. "Will you take her home with you, shelter her until she can forget this nightmare through which she's lived in pleasant dreams! You're my best friends-until she can tell whether-for me-it's real!"

"Jim!" Molly cried. "You know!"

Anderson laughed softly.

"To think, after all, it was on Captain's Island!"

They heard her descending the ladder. Molly went to meet her at the foot of the stairs. Miller led Anderson to the verandah.

They sat on the steps, watching the sky lighten for the birth of day, fresh, smiling, full of the health of youth. They roused themselves only when they heard the chugging of the gasolene launch. Then they walked to the pier and met the deputy sheriff and the rough native posse which Tony had brought from Sandport.

They answered the necessary questions. They told all they knew. They gave the sheriff the address of the hotel to which they would go in Martinsburg.

The sheriff left two of his party to take the fisherman and the woman to Sandport. He set out with the rest in the gasolene launch to explore the marsh channels to the north of the island.

"We've done all we can," Miller said. "Tony, get to the dingy and row out to the Dart Coax her engine and bring her around here. Andy, if she holds together, she'll have us in Martinsburg this afternoon. Bright lights, and the racket of life, and a real life ahead, if —"

He turned towards the house. Anderson put his arm around him.

"I don't think there are any 'ifs,' Jim."

Miller laughed a little.

"It's out of the way, Andy; it's hard to believe. She wouldn't yield that symbol of friendship and affection. I don't know her first name."

"You might find it convenient," Anderson said gravely. "I would ask her."

"Yes," Miller agreed.

He entered the plantation house, walked across the hall, and opened the library door. The girl sat in an easy chair turned towards the rear window. She gazed thoughtfully, sorrowfully over the black waste of the forest.

Molly had been sitting near her, but at Miller's entrance she arose and hurried past him. Miller heard her join Anderson on the porch. He closed the door softly. He walked towards the girl. She looked up, a little frightened, uncertain. He stood before her. He was ill-at-ease.

"You have never told me your first name," he said. "I understand why, but now-couldn't you?"

Her eyes were wide. The lines that had come into her face overnight softened. Her lips parted.

"You can ask that now! You care to know, after everything that has happened?"

"Yes, I care very much-all the more because of what has happened."

Her eyes were moist. She stammered a little.

"You're not just being kind! Oh, you wouldn't do that!"

"Only very selfishly," he answered.

"Then —" she said.

She reached up and drew his head close to her lips. Her lips moved.

He smiled and turned towards her lips.

www.ingramcontent.com/pod-product-compliance
Lightning Source LLC
LaVergne TN
LVHW020921200726
843506LV00011B/1752